THE SLEEP TRILOGY

Book III: Revelation

Peter Tennyson

ISBN-13: 978-0692111642 (Exodeye)
ISBN-10: 0692111646

Dedicated to Sara:
There's nothing more valuable than time,
and there's no one I'd rather share it with.

PROLOGUE: PHANTOMS & PHARMACEUTICALS

"What the hell am I doing here?!" demanded Brent with an aggravated snarl.

"I swear; I have no idea where he is," responded a stuttering orderly.

"No idea? You have no idea where he is?" the chief psychologist's anger was growing. *"So you let my patient escape?"*

"I have no idea where he went. He was here durin' lights out. I actually gave him a glass of water late at night. Said he couldn't sleep. Said the drugs were givin' him cottonmouth."

"So you went against protocol and let him out after giving him water?"

"No! He was in that cell when I walked away," the orderly asserted.

Dr. Sebastian Brent paced furiously throughout the now empty cell of Baxter Bishop, occasionally stopping to observe the surroundings in hope of finding some answer to the mysterious disappearance of his youngest patient. The cell was completely devoid of clues with the exception of a crudely-designed, stuffed decoy in the bed. Brent swiftly spun around and marched over to the cringing orderly. *"I'm going to make this simple for you. Was he here when your shift started?"*

The orderly hesitated as he nervously contemplated where this line of questioning would lead. *"Yeah, he was here. Came down from the common room."*

"*Good,*" Brent smiled. "*That makes this much easier.*"

"*Sir?*" the orderly responded with a confused tone.

"*The patient was here when you started the shift. Now, at the end of your shift, he is no longer here. Correct?*"

"*Yeah...*" mumbled the orderly.

"*So, I'm correct in ascertaining from you that this patient escaped from his locked cell during your shift?*"

"*Seems that way, I s'pose.*"

"*Yes, it does,*" Brent spat in an irritated manner as he bent down and inspected the cell door's lock. Shifting the lock back and forth to make sure it was functioning correctly, eventually the doctor turned to inspect the door frame for evidence of sabotage. He ran his finger down the door frame, pausing at the locking bar's slot which had been filled with a gooey, pink wad. "*Gum,*" breathed the doctor. "*He jammed the automated deadbolt with gum... and-*" the doctor dug his finger into the slot pulling out the disgusting wad, "*Gum and meds. He jammed the goddamn slot with gum and his meds...*" Brent rubbed his temple with his clean hand and turned to the orderly, "*When you gave him this cup of water, did you go into the cell?*"

The orderly furrowed his brow trying to remember the events of an evening that up until half an hour ago had seemed exhaustingly mundane. "*Uh, I guess when I opened the door, he was kinda standing where you are now, and I was in the hall with the cup.*"

"*So he was standing in the doorway when you gave him the water?*"

"*Yessir.*"

"*Well that explains pretty much everything here,*" Brent muttered with an exasperated edge to his voice. "*Paul!*"

"Yes sir?" another orderly stepped forward.

"Get me the surveillance footage of the front door, both interior and exterior cameras. I want to see when and where he went. It was a cold night last night. If he escaped the asylum, he couldn't have gotten far. Without his meds, I'm afraid he's going to rapidly decompensate."

"Yes sir," responded Paul with soldierly obedience.

"What would you like me to do now, sir?" softly asked the other orderly, hoping for a redeeming assignment.

"You?" laughed Brent. "I'm sorry, I thought that was clear an hour ago." Brent pulled a cigarette to his mouth and lit it with the natural fluidity of a downtown pool shark. "Get out of my sight. You're fired."

1

CHINESE FOOD

*"It is a great misfortune to be alone, my friends;
and it must be believed that solitude
can quickly destroy reason."*
- Jules Verne -

Two months had passed since Baxter escaped Hothrest Asylum. The final winter months had been a brutal ordeal, but in order to survive the icy season, he set up a small lean-to underneath a bridge several miles from the asylum and other authorities. Baxter's dealings with Cassius had become so frequent that his friend's absence was less common than his presence. The companionship was welcomed by Baxter, and with each passing day, his awareness that Cassius may be a figment of his imagination dwindled. The young man had no social interactions outside his bridge and had become quite the recluse, which led Cassius to jokingly refer to him as the modern version of a bridge troll.

Winter passed, and spring began thawing the layer of snow that still speckled the countryside. Over the last week, Baxter had become more brazen in his interactions with the world outside his underpass and had begun venturing into the nearby berg of Morristown.

Morristown had once been a bustling little city, but the dilapidated buildings littering main street and the rundown shops scattered through its downtown's perimeter were all demonstrative of a town that had fallen on harder times. Once a hub of the steel industry, Morristown's scenery was infected with abandoned foundries and the ruins of once profitable factories. The plan to set up camp in Morristown was, in Baxter's opinion, an ingenious decision. He had recalled the asylum superintendent, Dr. Sebastian Brent, complaining about crime in Morristown on numerous occurrences, and with the realization that he too would be identified as a fugitive, he decided to settle in the area where law enforcement would have the greatest preoccupation with others. In his outings throughout Morristown, Baxter quickly found he was well-informed of the town's criminal troubles but hadn't anticipated the influence the derelict and decaying society would have on him.

With the increasingly frequent conversations he'd have with Cassius, Baxter received many murmured criticisms from the local populace. Mothers with young children would securely hold them close as the young man joked and laughed with his imaginary friend, and his public displays of bizarre behavior quickly cultivated the stereotypical alienation frequently administered to the socially maladjusted. He would drink when he found reasonably clean water, and he'd eat when he found something that would not make him ill. His days were spent either foraging for sustenance or by long circular arguments with Cassius. Now that the winter had passed, he'd occasionally run across other down-and-out travelers to talk to, but there was little to be said. Between the orphanage and asylum, Baxter's last few years had been occupied with experiences that few could relate to.

It wasn't until a temperate mid-April evening that Baxter met his first sympathetic vagrant. His name was Scott, but his friends had given him the nickname "Stretch." Stretch was tall but only a year or so older than Baxter. His limbs were completely disproportionate with his body, and his coordination suffered greatly from the unusual ratio. Aside from his awkward length, Stretch was a handsome young man, who clearly could've been an individual of far greater means had his life not slipped into the gutters of society. The first time Baxter ran into Stretch was a rather embarrassing episode that took place as Baxter was dutifully sifting through a pile of refuse outside a Chinese restaurant on the outskirts of Morristown.

"So that's what desperate looks like," joked Stretch as he leaned against the brick wall of the alley. Baxter looked up briefly to identify the source of the ridicule before returning his attention to the garbage bin. He had grown accustomed to being the target of mockery from the town's residents and was certain he had no interest in engaging in a discussion with his rude, new acquaintance. However, regardless of Baxter's feelings, Stretch took a few steps closer to the garbage bin and peeked over the wall to view the contents. "This garbage isn't even fresh! You've got to be hungry," he said with a repulsed sneer.

"Don't you have something else you could be doing?" Baxter responded half-heartedly, still fully engrossed in his garbage-salvaging efforts.

"I s'pose so, but honestly, I've never felt as good with myself as I do right now. Hell, I'm not digging through an old shitty Chinese restaurant's dumpster for food. I'm going to go out on a limb here and assume you ain't got no home...am I right?"

Baxter didn't respond.

"You must *love* egg rolls," Stretch continued. "What would you do if you stumbled upon a whole tray full of half-eaten egg rolls?"

Baxter glared up at Stretch but said nothing.

"I bet if you came across those egg rolls, you'd just shit yourself with excitement, am I right?" By this point, Stretch had worked himself up into such hysterical laughter that he struggled to finish his comments amidst loud guffaws followed by gasps of breath. "If you want...you can come by my place sometime. I've got a nasty old sofa that I want to get rid of...don't have the wheels to take her to the dump...I'd let you eat it for free!" It was apparent that Stretch considered himself a great entertainer and wasn't going to be silenced by simple glares or ignored by silence. "Whew! I'm on a roll toda-" *Thwap!* A soggy egg roll slammed squarely against Stretch's cheek, launching a tiny amount of unknown sludge into his mouth. Stretch swiftly wiped his mouth and spat out onto the ground, "I'm gonna kill you!"

"Are you?" responded Baxter without a trace of concern in his voice. Are you gonna get in this dumpster and fight me because I finally shut you up?"

Scott's rage transformed into thought as he realized Baxter was indeed correct about predicting his opponent's unwillingness to fight in the garbage, "Get outta there, you little shit!"

"Yeah, I don't think I'm going to. I think I'm gonna stay right here in my dumpster with all this slimy goop coming up to my shins, and I'm going to laugh at you while you stand there and steam. Hell, I've got plenty more food in here I can throw." Baxter replied, lifting a handful of old noodles high into the air. "Hungry?"

"I swear to god, I'll kill you."

"You might, but you'll have to take a bath in about ten inches of - good God I don't even know what - before you do."

Stretch stood for a second clenching and unclenching his fists in a deep, rage-filled trance before reaching down and picking up the egg roll that had hit him. He threw the discarded missile at Baxter's head with a vicious growl. The lightly fried appetizer exploded against the wall a few feet from the dumpster-diver's head and launched chopped vegetable shrapnel everywhere.

"Stop destroying perfectly good food!" Baxter ordered with jocular solemnity. "You're ruining my lunch!"

Stretch's face turned bright red as he slowly recognized his helplessness in the repulsive situation in which he found himself. Noticing a small, white take-out box, he quickly snatched it up in his right hand and flung it at the dumpster. The box smashed against the opened top of the lid and a few pieces of an unknown entrée exploded over Baxter's head.

"Nooo," Baxter moaned with sardonic rue, "I was saving that for later!"

Stretch reached down and grabbed a much larger take-out box and cocked back his arm to launch another barrage of leftover Chinese gourmet, but then; he paused. "Saving that for later?" he mused pensively for a moment, and then, chuckled. Gradually, his chuckling evolved into a cackle, and then, became the same hysterical laughter that Baxter had earlier heard at his own expense. "Would you look at us!?"

Baxter looked down at himself covered in filth and then returned his view to Stretch. He smiled at his opponent, and both boys shared a bout of maniacal laughter at the ludicrousness of their behavior.

"What's your name, trash-hound?" Stretch asked once the laughter subsided.

"Baxter," responded the dumpster-diver.

"You want some real food?"

Baxter paused, still suspicious from the previous combat, "Yeah."

"Then get out of the garbage for shit's sake. I've got some that hasn't been in or around anyone else's mouth."

Baxter slowly threw one leg over the dumpster wall and reluctantly crawled out of his breakfast nook. "You aren't playing?" he asked suspiciously.

"I'm not playing, but if you don't get your ass out of there now, I'm outta here. I'm not standing around all day waiting for you to decide you don't want to stink like shit. Now, follow me."

The two boys passed through the decaying streets of the city they now called home. They passed numerous abandoned brick buildings that would have been condemned years ago in a more affluent town. Morristown, however, didn't have the funds necessary to demolish its decrepit older structures. So they remained, like Ozymandian reminders of a healthier past.

They continued on through the section of town that still held onto its struggling shops and collapsing homes until Stretch turned into a narrow alleyway and gestured for Baxter to follow him in a side door. The door took a few solid pushes from Stretch before the rusted hinges shrieked their admittance. Upon entering, Baxter was immediately taken aback by the smell of mildew and numerous other anonymous stenches, but he held his tongue, not wanting to offend his new host. "So this is my place," Stretch said with pride as he sat on an old plaid loveseat covered with massive holes oozing with stuffing. "Just a couple rooms. More than I need, really."

"Food?" Baxter reminded him.

"Oh yeah, right." Stretch reached over without getting up and popped open the top of a five-gallon bucket that used to contain washing detergent. Inside the bucket were numerous little snacks: half-eaten bags of potato chips, a few slices of old pepperoni pizza in a zip-lock bag, and countless different types of candy. The vibrant reds, yellows, and blues, of the Skittles and M&M's that littered the bottom of the bucket were a surreal image in the drab, dirty gray of the filthy apartment. "You can take anything but the pizza. I'm having that for dinner."

Baxter's hand begrudgingly passed over the zip-lock bag containing the pizza and moved onto one of the potato chip bags. "Thanks," he mumbled in between mouthfuls of crumbling chips. "I like your place."

Stretch glared at his guest for a moment silently measuring whether or not there was any sarcasm in Baxter's voice. After deciding the comment was genuine in its complimentary nature, he laughed, "Yeah, I like it. Let's me do my own shit. Don't have to answer to no one."

"I camp out over by the bridge passed that bar, Ed's, on the corner."

"The bridge over Lawson's Creek?" asked Stretch.

"I guess. It's not too far from town, and it gives me my alone time."

"That's what it's about, man," laughed Stretch. "You get high?"

"High? What do you mean?"

Stretch smiled wryly at his guest before reaching under the cushion of his loveseat and pulling out a purple, velvet bag with the words *Crown Royal* embroidered on it. From the bag, Stretch extracted a small, glass pipe and a couple of thin vials. The contents of the bag were particularly well taken care of compared to everything else in the apartment. As dust and grime were allowed to settle on every surface in his home, Stretch kept his narcotic paraphernalia immaculately cleaned and in mint condition.

"What's that?" questioned Baxter quietly.

"Some stuff my friend gave me. Really good stuff. Makes you feel like you're in Heaven."

"How do you know what it's like to be in Heaven?" returned Baxter.

Stretch laughed while packing a crystalline substance from the vial into the small, glass pipe, "I don't know man. I mean it feels like everything's going good. You ever feel like everything is just shit?"

"For most of my life, all I can remember is everything being shit."

"This stuff-" Stretch began but interrupted himself in order to take a long slow drag from the pipe. "This stuff makes all of that go away." As he exhaled a lingering trail of smoke, he smiled, but the expression seemed different to Baxter. The warmth that usually inhabits the eyes of anyone smiling was absent, and he found it eerie that the mouth seemed to convey a different expression than the eyes, as if true contentment had been gained, but something else, some intangible quality, had been allowed to escape. Stretch trembled, *"It is soooo good."* He handed the pipe to Baxter, who took it in his hand carefully and inspected it with dubious eyes.

"I don't think so, Stretch," he responded. "Thanks for the offer, but I have a bad history with drugs."

"Sounds like you have a bad history with shit," Stretch chuckled. "*This?* This takes care of all that. Don't take a big hit or anything. Just a tiny little-" he inhaled rapidly and abruptly stopped. "Trust me, man. I wouldn't give you my food and then try and hurt you." He put the pipe up to Baxter's mouth, "Real quick." He lit the pipe and repeated the rapid inhaling noise.

Baxter breathed in quickly and looked at Stretch for further instruction.

"Hold it in," the older boy coached. "One...two... three...four-"

2

A WARM OCEAN WITH COLD WAVES

Baxter tried his best to hold in the smoke, but he eventually exploded in a coughing fit.

"Woo! Good!" Stretch exclaimed clapping, "Nice! Now, how does that feel?"

Baxter didn't answer immediately. He felt a warm blanket wrap around his mind, and a wave of euphoria wash over his entire body. He breathed out normally, but the breath seemed to take its time, casually flowing out of his mouth like it was strolling on the air currents of the room. *"Wow,"* Baxter rasped.

"I know, right?" smiled Stretch. "Now lie back and relax."

Baxter leaned back on the dilapidated loveseat and, now, admired its comfort. The fabric that looked and felt so coarse now seemed like the smoothest satin, and Baxter found himself repeatedly adjusting for the tactile sensation.

He closed his eyes and felt a soft, gentle electricity push through his body. It started from his chest and pulsed outward to his extremities. With each wave of joyful electricity, he felt more comfortable and sank deeper into the couch. After several minutes, he felt a manic energy shoot through his arms and legs, and he quickly jumped off the couch to his feet. "Wow, I feel incredible! What is this stuff?"

"Good, right?" Stretch laughed at the narcotic naivety of his guest. "Always makes me feel like running around downtown like a maniac."

"I'm down."

Stretch laughed, "Nah, you don't actually want to. I did it once. I sprinted to the other side of town. Then, I came down. You do not want to be on the other side of town when you come down. Once you come down, there's nothing you'll want more than this couch."

"I feel like my blood has been replaced with soda," Baxter laughed with excitement.

"Told ya. Heaven," stated Stretch with a matter of fact tone. The host's face was now beginning to lose its jubilance, and the broad smile had wilted into a relaxed but emotionless stare.

Finally, Baxter too, felt the euphoric state beginning to wither. The pulsing source from his chest had slowed, and the pleasant waves of euphoria were becoming noticeably less frequent.

"Here it comes," yawned Stretch.

"Here what comes?"

"This is why you don't run to the other end of town. Get ready to feel like a slug."

Baxter felt his energy level dipping as he yawned in turn. In less than an hour, the two young men fell asleep in the comforting arms of the worn-out couch.

The first thing Baxter recognized in the dream were the familiar blue eyes and golden hair of Eliza. The two orphans sat on an old railway bridge overlooking a picturesque mountain stream. Their bare feet dangled over the side of the old track and kicked back and forth over the creek that churned many feet below. Mountains reached up to the sky all around them, and the height of the peaks immediately reminded Baxter of the incredibly high bookshelves of the dream library.

Eliza let out a girlish laugh and inconspicuously allowed her left foot to graze up against Baxter's. She hooked her arm in his and drew herself closer to the young man. "Do you think we'll ever be free?" she asked with her sapphire eyes staring intently into his.

"Free?" Baxter questioned, still acclimating to the dreamscape.

"Yeah, free. I mean free from everything that shouldn't be our problems. Free from all the things that weren't our fault."

"I don't understand," the young man responded smiling happily just to spend time with the girl he desired more than anything. "What things that weren't our fault?"

"Everything!" was the girl's response. "Why do such terrible things have to happen to people that never wanted anything but good to surround them?"

Baxter didn't answer but continued to gaze admiringly at his companion.

Eliza seemed oblivious to the brazen stare of Baxter as she continued, "I mean, so much of what happens seems to be completely out of our control, and then, we face the consequences for things we didn't want to happen in the first place. It just seems that for us, the world is unfair. Not unfair in the childish way, but deeply unfair. As if we're being judged for the effects of others' actions on us."

Eventually, Baxter was able to break his trance-like gape and respond to the girl, "You understand my pain more than anyone ever has. I know this is a dream, and you're not really you, but I suppose this is the part of you I like to imagine existing. Every day I wish more than anything in the world, I could speak to you about that day. About the terrible thing that I did, and about how sorry I am that it happened. It's funny that you bring up consequences because for the longest time they were what upset me the most. They were the things I found the most unfair. Every morning I'd wake up and think about how I'd never be able to touch you again, and all because of something that I couldn't control. I'd never be able to speak to you again. Never be able to hear you talk to me. There were nights in Hothrest I'd just lie on my bed and think about how much I missed just hearing your voice. The way your breath would tickle my ear when you whispered to me. But as the months passed, and I'd stay awake thinking about you, my perspective changed. It wasn't the consequences that continued to upset me. It was the weakness that I couldn't tell you the truth. I felt so evil because of what happened, I couldn't bring myself to ever speak to you again. Every time Sansarev came to visit me, I thought about sending a letter to you back with him, but I never had the courage to do it. My cowardice, that is the part I hated the most. I don't accept all the responsibility for what happened. I don't think I could live with myself if I actually did. But my fear I do live with, and every day I think about how pathetic I am for losing you."

A train whistle roared in the distance. The loud noise seemed to surround the couple as it echoed off the surrounding mountains. Baxter looked in every direction for the approach of a train, but Eliza seemed content in ignoring the locomotive's scream. Her eyes picked up a reflection of sunlight from the stream as they returned the romantic gaze back into Baxter's. She reached a hand out and pulled the young man's face towards hers. She pulled his head close and pressed her lips against his for several seconds. "I wish you didn't think you'd lost me. I wish you'd come back to me," she whispered in his ear.

Baxter felt the sensation of her breath in his ears again, and it drove him wild. He gently touched her leg and kissed her, but upon touching her lips, the train whistle repeated its shriek. Now, the loud blast came from a much closer distance. The sound was deafening and caused Baxter to quickly spin around, scanning the dreamscape for its source. As his head turned, he saw the train still a couple hundred meter away but rapidly approaching the bridge.

He turned to Eliza one last time, but the girl's form was a bizarre blur. Baxter reached out and held her arm, but the girl's shape continued to wave and distort in an ominous manner. The train let out another shrill blast, and the sound of steel wheels grating against rusted track resonated throughout the scenic dreamscape.

"Eliza!" shouted Baxter as he shook the blurry apparition's arm. The young man screamed, "We have to get out of here!" and heard his words echoing off the surrounding mountains, but Eliza made no response. Instead, the now rippling illusion slowly began to establish a more temporal form, but the form that was coming into existence caused even greater uneasiness in the young man. He continued to hold the arm, but his eyes grew wider in an excited terror when he first recognized his mother's eyes staring back at him. They were wide in horror, and she pointed behind him at the incoming locomotive. Baxter, once again, quickly turned his head to measure the train's distance, but upon turning, recognized there were merely seconds before the train would reach him. He turned back to his mother and shouted, "You are not here! You must leave now!" Her soft blue eyes glistened brightly for just a second. Baxter couldn't help but marvel at their tenderness and beauty, and for a moment, he couldn't remember seeing them so vividly. As quickly as the ephemeral apparition had previously blurred, once again it began to shift out of the dream world. The train let out one last terrifying warcry before Baxter pushed himself from the railway bridge and fell for what felt like minutes before hitting the surface of the creek. The cold, spring water washed over the young man and sent chilling sensations through his body. As the temperature casused the young man's extremities to throb in the icy water, Baxter closed his eyes and chose to wake.

When Baxter awoke, his eyes darted around the apartment. The high from Stretch's drug left, and as rapidly as the blissful rush overcame him, a darkness began to creep into the periphery of his sight. The dingy apartment's shadows seemed more malevolent than they had upon his arrival. They now appeared to grow larger with every passing second until they threatened to envelop the couch in their surreal darkness. From where Baxter lay, the shadows slowly edged toward him like the teeth of a great, dark wolf preparing to devour the room whole. Stretch was still awkwardly splayed out fast asleep on the couch and had created a small pool of drool on the armrest. Baxter just sat with his paranoia building, unsure whether or not he should wake his host and inform him of the impending doom that would certainly visit them should they stay on the couch. Eventually, his fear of Stretch's anger at being awoken and his paranoia of the growing shadows caused him to rise and cautiously evacuate the ramshackle apartment.

Once outside, Baxter found that dusk had arrived, and Morristown was now shrouded in darkness save a few strategically placed street lights shining over the intersections. It has been said that some derelict sections of cities look better in the dark, but in Morristown, that was not the case. The shadows falling on the abandoned shops and factories exacerbated the town's deteriorated appearance. Occasionally, Baxter would notice a fellow vagrant quickly traversing a dim city street or rummaging for supplies in a bar alley, but they were of little concern to him now. The comedown from his activities with Stretch left him in a treacherous psychological conundrum. He was caught between terrible loneliness and a fear of everyone around him. Whether under the quiet glow of a lamppost or slipping through the streets at night unnoticed, there was a severe paranoia gradually growing inside Baxter's mind. Frequently, the young man found himself looking over his shoulder or avoiding eye contact with anyone around him for fear of being recognized.

The only person he felt he could trust was Cassius, who like Baxter's dreams, seemed always available to him when needed.

"Those drugs back there; that felt great," Baxter laughed.

"Yeah, I bet, but don't get caught up in a new world until we've found out what we need to know," Cassius responded politely as he plodded alongside his friend.

"What do you mean what we need to know?"

"We didn't get out of Hothrest to sit under a bridge and do drugs with the skid marks of this shit town."

"Hey, I'm surviving."

"Barely."

"What do you suggest we do then?" questioned Baxter angrily.

"Schaffer or Eliza. Take your pick," returned Cassius.

Baxter froze at the mention of Eliza's name. It felt so bizarre to hear it spoken by someone else's voice. After several moments of silence, he spat on the ground and answered, "I can't see Eliza. I don't know what to say to her yet."

"Good."

"How's that good?"

"It settles it then," smiled Cassius. "If we can't see Eliza, we deal with Schaffer."

"How do you figure we do that?"

"First, we can simply pay her a visit. In the morning we head to her office."

"If we're caught, they'll drag us back to Hothrest."

Cassius chuckled dryly, "*If* they catch us, they'll drag us to the Morristown pen, kid. I'd wager to say Hothrest Asylum is behind us regardless of how this plays out."

Baxter raised his head and looked off into the distance. The bridge that hid his camp was now visible, and he slowly made his way down along the side of the creek. When the actual camp came into sight, Baxter noticed his lean-to was not in the same condition that he'd left it. The tarp he'd used to provide shelter had been stolen, and the wooden stakes he'd salvaged from the surrounding woods had been pulled from the ground. He noticed one stake had been javelined into the creek and was protruding from the water about six feet in. The rest was nowhere to be seen. An old canvas bag he'd been storing miscellaneous supplies in had also been stolen.

"Aghhh!" he screamed as he fell to his knees. The shout echoed off the steel beams above and the concrete buttresses that surrounded him.

"This looks much worse than it actually is," coaxed Cassius from behind him. "Keep in mind, we didn't really have anything of value. This was all just a bit of work that we can redo easily."

"I don't want to redo it! I'm tired of being shit on every time I turn around! I'm tired of being the world's punching bag!"

"It's springtime, and the weather is perfect. Let's just get some rest and deal with this tomorrow," Cassius said hoping to placate the young man, but Baxter, exhausted from the anxiety and drugs, had already huddled down against one of the concrete walls and was well on his way to falling asleep. Cassius paced for a few moments before lying down on the other side of the camp. "Tomorrow, we go see Schaffer."

3

RETURN TO SCHAFFER

Morning brought beams of sunlight into the destroyed camp under the causeway and caused the ransacked base to become rather picturesque. The rays reflecting off the creek bounced up to the underbelly of the causeway causing beautifully luminous, web-like refractions to sparkle and dance on the dirty concrete above. Baxter lay on the ground and admired the natural kaleidoscope taking place overhead, but it wasn't long before Cassius reminded him they had business to attend to.

"You can daydream later, kid. We have a ways to go to get to Schaffer's place."

"I'm not sure we should be going there," Baxter replied yawning.

"We'll be fine. We can hitchhike to the town and just stay on foot from there. You don't wanna know what she's gotta say?"

"I seriously doubt she's gonna tell us anything except that she's called the police."

Cassius adjusted his weight and propped his elbow up against the wall, "You honestly think she's going to call the police? You remember Caine. They were *already* looking into her. I think you're crazy thinkin' Schaffer wants the police involved in anything she's doing."

Baxter stood up and brushed some dirt off his pants. "I guess you're right. I'm not even sure what I'd say to her."

"Well, she knows you've escaped so you won't have to fill her in there. I'm sure her office was one of the first places the cops checked out after you turned up missing from Hothrest."

"I wouldn't care at all about that. I just don't know what I'd ask her about my father. How did she know him? Was she sleeping with him?" Baxter reached up and rubbed his forehead. "In the end, I just want to understand why my parents are dead."

"And she's the only one who can answer that for you."

"You're right, I know," Baxter finally admitted. "When we're done we should stop by Stretch's and get some food."

"I'm not sure about him," replied Cassius suspiciously. "Let's just play it by ear."

Baxter nodded and brushed some more dirt off his shirt. He spat in his hand and ran it through his hair which was the longest it had ever been. He looked down in the creek's current and found a much older reflection than he'd expected. He reached his hands down into the stream's cool, clear water and began washing his face. He knew he'd have to look as presentable as possible if he had any hope of catching a ride to the office where so many questions began. After completing some basic grooming in the stream, the young man climbed the bank to the causeway road and turned his thumb in the direction he wished to travel. Several cars passed without interest in picking up the haggard hitchhiker before a beat up old, red truck lurched to a stop along the side of the road. An older man who looked equally haggard as the homeless young orphan rolled down the window, looked the boy up and down with a judicious glare, grunted affirmatively, and nodded his head to the truck bed. Baxter didn't hesitate in fear the driver may rethink his decision and swiftly jumped up into the back of the old vehicle.

As the truck took off down the road, the sensation of wind whipping his hair left Baxter with an ambivalent feeling of freedom mixed with quiet anxiety. A calm introspection swept over the young man as he watched the trees and shrubs littering the roadside flash by in a continuing blur of lush greens. For the first time in his memory, he felt a kinship with nature. The wilderness wouldn't judge him; it just passed by in innocuous indifference.

He spent the next several minutes relaxing to the engine's clunky growling as it lumbered down the road. The old man in the truck cab paid him no mind but periodically slapped his hand against the roof as his stereo blared a distorted rendition of Lynyrd Skynyrd's *Simple Man* from broken speakers. Baxter didn't want to be dropped off directly at Schaffer's office as he believed an advantage could be gained from surprising his old therapist. When the old truck roared down the closest road to the office, he stood up in the bed and gently tapped his hand on the roof of the cabin. The engine's growl became labored before it transformed into a loud, rhythmic purr beneath the hood. He carefully jumped from the side of the rusted, red pickup and waved thankfully at the driver who in turn nodded with only the slightest expression of bewilderment. Baxter had elected to be dropped off at what appeared a most unusual location. There was nothing but affluent residential homes and forests at the intersection, but the worn out pickup coughed down the road without any further questions.

Baxter knew Schaffer's office was still a decent trek, but he knew a large pickup pulling into her office driveway would forfeit the possibility of surprise. The young man walked down the street at a brisk pace, playing over in his head the questions he intended to ask his former therapist.

"Why were you writing to my father?" Baxter muttered under his breath. "Were you sleeping with him? Do you know why they were killed?" Even though the wound was old, Baxter could still feel his eyes begin to mist up every time he thought about his parents, and specifically, his mother. He remembered looking into her haunting eyes as he sat on the train track. He wished he could've stayed on the railway bridge longer and just talked to her. He missed his family dearly.

When he finally caught sight of Schaffer's building, he was unpleasantly surprised by several cars crowding the parking lot. There were no police vehicles, which was a relief, but he hadn't intended on such a large audience when he finally got the chance to question the doctor. As he neared the building, he realized the situation was even worse than he'd anticipated. Once at the front door, he looked at the plaque on the wall beside the entrance way that used to contain the name "Dr. Veronica Schaffer" in an elegant, formal font. The plaque had been pried off, and a new, metallic sign took its place that read, "J. Rockcliff, Luxury Real Estate Offices."

Baxter gently pushed the door open with uncertainty, half-expecting to find the portly Ms. McDaniel's sitting behind her desk, but once the door had swung open, a completely alien scene greeted the young man. The front room that used to be a reception and waiting area was completely empty save a few awkwardly placed paintings on the walls. The young man poked his head inside the door frame and looked around the interior of the office.

"Can I...help you?" asked an opulently dressed older man. He looked Baxter up and down before quivering his snow white moustache in derision at the young vagrant. I'm not sure where you think you are, but I can assure you; *you're not there.*"

"Ms....Doc...Doctor Schaff...?" the young man mumbled with a clumsy tongue.

"Dr. Veronica Schaffer, I presume?" the older man snickered victoriously at his delicious parody.

"Yea - yes."

"Well," he straightened his moustache in an attempt to look menacing. "Dr. Schaffer does not work in this building anymore. The type of individuals that she worked with are not in this building anymore. And the people *in* this building? *We* do not want *that* population near *J. Rockcliff's Real Estate Offices.*"

"Where ... where did she go?" Baxter asked in a stunned manner.

"I do not know where she has departed to, sir, but I can assure you she is not here. I would most certainly appreciate it if you yourself departed." By this point, the little man had grown into a heated exasperation and began shuffling his feet in an anxious manner.

Baxter slowly back out the front door and stood puzzled on the front walkway. He caught a reflection of himself in the window and immediately understood the cause of the older man's aggravation. Given the circumstances Baxter felt he had done a respectable job cleaning up, but at second glance into his reflection, he realized that his clothes were in terrible condition. His shirt was badly stained, and he had two shallow cuts on either side of his neck just above the collarbone. His pants had several stains from either mud or blood, and his knees were visible through two large holes on either pant leg. His disheveled reflection in the window caught him off guard. He angled his nose to his armpit and timidly sniffed then recoiled immediately at the putrid aroma that permeated his nostrils. From his peripheral, he caught the repulsed look of the older man who was still watching him from inside the building. The man sneered with repugnance while making shooing motions with both hands. Baxter took another series of steps back and turned to head to the street. He felt lost and confused. He had not anticipated the absence of Schaffer and was left completely uncertain of his next step. With none of his questions answered, and the unusual absence of Cassius, Baxter decided to return to the only place that sounded familiar to him, Stretch's apartment. He knew it would be a long walk, but he also knew in an upper class neighborhood such as this, he wouldn't easily find a ride hitchhiking. He hit the road and headed back towards Morristown, only looking back once at his therapist's old office.

4

BROKEN BONES

The trek back to downtown Morristown took Baxter the better part of three hours, but his legs were in good shape from roaming the streets for the past couple months. Eventually, he reached Stretch's door in the late afternoon and knocked quietly while calling his friend's name. There was no answer at the door and no discernible sounds from inside. He knocked again with much greater assertion and waited for a response, but none came.

"He must be out scoring more drugs," Cassius commented with a wry grin.

"Who knows what he's doing?" Baxter defended.

"Well, we know he's not out rummaging for food. Wouldn't want to get dirty."

"I guess we wait."

"What about Schaffer?" Cassius prodded.

"What about her? We went to her office. She's moved

out. Gone. I don't know how to find her. I can't ask the cops."

"So, you're not going to search for her anymore?"

"I'm trying to survive. If I find any clue about where she is, then I'll investigate, but for now, I'm just going to relax here until Scott shows up." Baxter fell back against the grungy wall and slid down until he was sitting on the street.

"Fine. You stay here, I'm going to find some food," Cassius said as he walked away from Stretch's door.

Baxter waited for about an hour outside the apartment. The sun had just begun to set, and the orange hues of evening light stopped at the narrow street's entrance. A small group of men in their early twenties came into view from around the corner and hesitated briefly when they noticed Baxter. Whatever conversation they had been involved in before seeing the young man came to an abrupt halt and was replaced with quiet gestures and mocking laughter. As the group grew closer, Baxter felt the hairs on the back of his neck perk up in alarm. He was still seated beside Stretch's door, but as it was located at the end of the alleyway, he realized he had no way to escape from any unfortunate misunderstanding that may arise. He looked into the eyes of the young men that approached him and immediately wished he had an option for retreat.

"I've seen you 'round," smiled one of the young men in front with a mischievous grin. He wore black jeans and an oversized, white t-shirt that looked severely stretched at the neck. From what Baxter could gather, he appeared to be the de facto leader of the group. "I saw you stumblin' outta Stretch's hole the other day."

"I was just-" Baxter began to answer but was cut off.

"I only know one reason why anyone would be stumblin' outta Stretch's hole. They either grabbin' money or holdin' drugs. Now which you doin', sweetheart? Ya got cash on you...? Or you holdin' some rocks for me?"

Baxter took a couple of steps backward as the group's leader advanced. He felt ashamed of the cowardice in his voice as he responded, "I–I don't have either. I hung out with Stretch the other day and just wanted to see if he was still around."

"You ain't got no money?"

Baxter shook his head.

"Drugs?"

Baxter remained silent. Without command, the other members of the gang began to spread out to block any path that would allow Baxter through them. He realized that if he gave them nothing, he would more than likely be attacked, and with nothing in his possession they desired, Baxter felt his hands involuntarily clench as he continued to step back towards the end of the alley.

"Oh man! Looks like you're a smart boy. Ya got the idea real quick." The leader took three rapid steps advancing which caused Baxter to quickly ready his fists in preparation for the fight. The leader stopped when he saw Baxter's clenched fists rise, and he laughed, "Whoa! Check this kid out, guys! You going to fight *all* of us?"

"Don't want to," Baxter responded through grit teeth. "Just want to go home."

The leader let out a loud guffaw, "You smell like shit! Pretty sure you ain't got a home. But don't worry, we goin' to take care of ya." He nodded to the other members of his crew, and the semi-circle they had formed slowly began converging on Baxter.

"*HEL-*" Baxter tried to cry out, but he was immediately struck in the stomach, knocking the wind out of him. He fell to the ground and gasped for air while both hands held his midsection.

"Help! Help!" cried the gang leader sardonically. "Oh please, someone! *Anyone!?*" The rest of the gang snickered at their captain's ridicule.

"Stay away from me!" Baxter snarled as he slowly gripped an empty beer bottle in his hand.

"I'll stay away, but I can't make any promises for these guys," the leader joked. He turned and began walking through the group, "Kick the ever-loving shit out of this punk. When you're done, if I have to hear him cry, I'm going to kill him."

The first member of the crew stepped forward with both fists clenched, and a look of diabolic depravity twinkling in his eyes.

Baxter chose not to wait to defend himself. As soon as the first aggressor stepped forward, Baxter lunged forward recklessly swinging the beer bottle down on his opponent. The beer bottle connected solidly with the left temple of the gang member and shattered into a chaotic constellation of glass. Although his assailant dropped like a sack of flour into a muddy pool of grime, the rest of the gang became incensed with the incapacitation of their comrade. Baxter barely had time to shield his face before the other men had mauled him. He felt sharp, stinging blows coming from every direction as the gang mercilessly delivered kicks and punches to every inch of his body. A fist struck him in the side of the jaw causing an audible click as he felt his mandible detach. Another fist struck the side of his face and caused the fractured jaw to simply hang loose from his mouth. One of the gang members continually drove his knee into Baxter's stomach until there was no more air to knock out of the young man. The only thing that raced through his mind was whether or not he would survive the beating. Each punch or kick slid his body on the filthy pavement of the alleyway until it stopped.

Baxter felt no more blows striking him. Pain throbbed throughout his entire body, and he desperately wanted to be unconscious, but his wishes weren't answered. He rolled his head to the side to determine what his attackers were doing. They had stepped back a few paces and were laughing with each other and congratulating one another for thoroughly pulverizing their victim. The member who had been dispatched by Baxter's beer bottle had now regained his feet and was switching shoes with another of the gang members. In Baxter's discombobulated state, he couldn't really comprehend what was going on around him. The voices laughing and joking were completely indiscernible and incomprehensible to him as he felt his limp jaw rest against the street pavement.

He felt a breath in his ear that was facing skyward, "I'm going to feel that bottle for weeks, you sunnuvabitch. That's ok though, ya know. Cause you're going to feel this for the rest of your fucking life. See this?" he asked as he stepped down in front of Baxter's face with the boots he borrowed from his colleague. He kneeled down and tapped on the tip of the boot with his right hand demonstrating its steel-toed construction. Baxter's eyes closed as he realized what was coming. All he could do was pray to any god that would listen.

"I don't want to die," he whimpered.

"I don't want you to die, either," claimed the man that hovered over his body. "I want you to suffer for the rest of your life, and *this* should do it."

The gang member took a few steps back and then ran forward kicking with all his weight and strength square into the side of Baxter's torso. The expulsion of breath was audible to everyone spectating the gruesome event, and the cracking of bone was accompanied by cheers and congratulations amongst the thugs. The last thing Baxter remembered was the final graces of sunlight being eclipsed by the boot of the laughing man above him. The shadow covered his face, and then, the boot fell with crushing force down on his skull.

5

ESCAPING DARKNESS

The rain came down in violent sheets as the wind gusted in and out of the downtown alleyways. All the streetlights intermittently pulsed on and off leaving a crescent moon as the only reliable source of light. Periodic bolts of lightning danced across the night sky serving as accompaniment to the flashing light provided by the malfunctioning street lamps.

Underneath one of the streetlights about thirty meters away, Baxter saw the blurry silhouette of a figure braving the weather in a thick trench coat. The wind was perpetually whipping the coat wildly around the figure, but the body didn't budge or sway in the violent gusts. It stood stalwart and unmoving like a cliff-perched lighthouse braving a violent deluge.

Baxter stepped out into the street and felt the wind rush against his body as he attempted to walk towards the solitary figure. Each step he took seemed to take more effort than the last as the sheets of rain ripped across the downtown neighborhood. Thunder boomed overhead, but on the street level, it sounded like a soft, distant drum as it competed with the torrential storm. With every few steps, Baxter was forced to reach up and wipe the rain from his face in order to see a few feet in front of him. Everything was flooded by the storm, but the figure illuminated by the pulsing streetlight remained steadfast in the squall.

When Baxter finally reached the figure, it seemed oblivious to his presence. There was no reaction of any kind. The figure remained completely motionless, and for a moment, Baxter doubted whether it was human at all or some bizarre robed statue. He called out to the figure which was only a few feet from him, but there was no response. He saw the outline of a face but none of the typical features one would expect. The face was still difficult to discern due to the intense rainfall, but as Baxter drew closer, an expression of horror slowly washed over his own face.

The unknown figure's face was ghoulishly deformed. Each human feature that could even be mildly discerned was swollen to hideous proportions and barely resembled the original.

"Hello?" Baxter called to the figure, but there was no response. *"Hello?"* he attempted again, but still, the face made no expression that it even registered Baxter's existence. He drew closer to the figure until he was just a foot from the statuesque figure's visage, and he abruptly realized what he was looking at.

6

ESCAPING LIGHT

His facial features were obscured by both the filth of the mud puddle in which the reflection was captured as well as the severe contusions that covered his face. Both eyes were swollen shut from the beatings, and his jaw, which had been severely injured, hung awkwardly from his head. At first, he tried slowly adjusting his body, but pain immediately began emanating from his rib cage. He gently lowered his right arm and lifted his shirt to discover the majority of his torso had already turned to a blackened purple. Even the slightest movement caused numerous, relentless waves of pain to wash over the young man's entire body. For the better part of an hour, Baxter simply lay there, frightened of exacerbating a wound that he hadn't yet discovered. Eventually, Baxter shuffled his legs out from under him and attempted to stand. The pain was excruciating, but he knew he had to escape the downtown area. His position was futile. He couldn't go to the police, or he'd eventually be identified and taken to prison, and he couldn't stay on the streets because of the gangs. Even if he survived this last encounter, he didn't imagine the thugs that had left him within inches of his life would be very merciful if they found him again.

After numerous failures to rise, he stumbled forward and forced himself to lean against the brick wall of the alley. Luckily, his legs hadn't been badly injured in the assault, and at this point, they were the only part of his body that didn't rebel against his slightest movements with sharp throbbing pain. While using the wall to balance, he slowly slid his way towards the front of the alley. If only he could reach his camp, he could take his time with recovery. His stomach rumbled, and although he hadn't eaten in a day, the pangs of hunger were inconsequential when compared to the wounds of his beating. After a tortuous journey, Baxter reached the mouth of the narrow alley that had nearly served as his coffin. He looked in both directions outside the alley to make sure his assailants were out of the area before dragging himself out onto the sidewalk. Numerous unsuspecting citizens of Morristown stared at the broken young man with varying expressions ranging from pitying suspicion to overt repulsion. The town's economic recession combined with the penitentiary's influence left the townspeople dubious of strangers, especially those that appeared to be part of the gritty underbelly that had been blossoming recently in the urban sections of Morristown. A stocky mother in her mid-forties passed by with her young son and pulled him close to her as they passed Baxter. She glared up menacingly at the young man before tugging her child and mumbling judgments about the "shape of the world these days."

Baxter hadn't been standing in front of the alleyway for more than fifteen minutes before a police cruiser appeared. The officer slowed to a crawl as he carefully studied the badly beaten young man, and all Baxter could do was close his eyes and hope. He didn't know if it was possible for him to escape from a cop given his current circumstances. He deliberately flexed his leg muscles to see if they even had the strength to flee, and although they weren't seriously injured themselves, the rest of his body trembled with agony when they felt his legs struggle to stabilize. The cruiser slowly moved on past Baxter, but just as the young man began to breathe a sigh of relief, the vehicle pulled over to the side of the road, and the driver's side door opened. Baxter knew he'd have no opportunity to escape the officer once confronted. From such short range, either pepper spray or a well thrown baton could end any hope for flight given his severely injured condition. He had no choice; he decided to begin his flight immediately. As inconspicuously as possible, the young man began hobbling down the sidewalk in the opposite direction of the parked cruiser. He did his best to walk without any noticeable struggles that may cause the officer to become suspicious, but the constant suffering that pulsed through his upper body caused his gait to intensely tremble. He hadn't limped more than several meters before he heard the officer behind him.

"Excuse me, son. May I have a word with you?" the officer called with a thick accent. Baxter continued walking, pretending not to hear the officer's request. "Sir, I'm going to need you to hang on a second." Baxter heard the officer's hard sole footsteps begin to hasten slightly, and he too quickened his pace. "Sir! I need you to slowly turn around! You know I'm talking to you! Do not ignore me!"

At this point, Baxter found very little recourse and commenced, to the best of his ability, a sprint down the sidewalk. He strained to keep his swollen eyes open as he searched for a possible escape, but the swelling made it nearly impossible to open either eye to its fullest.

"Son of a bitch!" the officer snarled behind him and began pursuit.

Adrenaline rushed through Baxter. The mixture of horrible pain and desperation surged throughout the young man's body as he did his best to elude the officer. After a block, he took a sharp right into a shopping center and continued to dash through the sparsely populated parking lot. A few seconds later as the officer turned the same corner, he cried out another warning, *"Freeze, or I'll shoot!"*

"Please hit me in the head," Baxter mumbled under his breath as he continued running through the other side of the shopping center. Although he was terrified of actually being shot, he didn't believe the officer would fire on him with no real threat or actual cause for arresting him, and the officer didn't. He simply gasped out a couple more expletives and street names into his shoulder radio while continuing his chase.

Tears poured out of Baxter's eyes as he struggled to stay upright despite the crippling anguish radiating from his badly wounded ribs and jaw. He contemplated turning on the officer and attacking just to get the bullet that would end the pain, but the fear of the undiscovered country kept him running.

Once he cleared the shopping center parking lot and another short alleyway, Baxter began glancing over his shoulder to evaluate how far back the officer was in his pursuit. Although no longer in sight, Baxter could still hear the officer barking out commands into his radio. It wouldn't be long before backup arrived, and the young man knew he had no hope of outrunning the cars once they showed up. His entire body was rebelling, and only adrenaline was enabling his retreat. If he had any hope of escape, he'd have to find a place to hide soon.

"Just a little further," Baxter encouraged himself breathing heavily. "...Just a little further." He turned another corner and hobbled off towards a vacant lot that was heavily overgrown with brush and speckled with some small abandoned houses. Once he reached the empty lot, he scanned the area for anywhere suitable to hide. He could no longer hear the officer's heavy steps or loud, radio commands and determined this was his chance to vanish.

He found a large pile of construction debris in one corner of the lot and began digging himself underneath several large sheets of particleboard. Entrenching himself in the pile of debris required the use of his upper body, and

every movement of his arms caused an excruciating stinging to overcome his entire body. He couldn't complain,
and he couldn't rest. In a few short moments, he'd lever-
aged himself underneath the pile of debris. There were
numerous nails protruding from various sized planks, and
Baxter cautiously maneuvered inside to further remove
himself from view. Eventually, the red and blue lights of
the police backup flashed throughout the neighborhood
and painted the run-down shop and apartment walls with
their sirens. Baxter remained as still and quiet as possible
in his hiding spot for over an hour while a handful of officers half-heartedly searched the area. The young man felt
a refreshing wave of relief wash over him as soon as he
realized there were no canine units to help the officers
with their search.

Two hours passed underneath the construction pile. The
cramped space had worsened Baxter's pain, and he began
to feel faint from the toll on his body. He placed a broken
four by four down into the ground and used it to lever two
of the heavy boards off the pile. Even the modest amount
of pressure required to shift the boards caused his ribs to
sting, but once the pile groaned and the boards gave way,
the young man was finally able to escape his dangerous
sanctuary.

Baxter did his best to brush off the dirt and sawdust,
but he knew the majority of mud and filth had stained

his clothes, and his quest for cleanliness was a futile one. He kept to the edges of the vacant lot and resorted to stealthily glancing around building corners to be certain the police presence had departed. After several minutes, he leaned against the brick wall of the tenement adjacent to his empty lot and sunk to the ground. The pain was gradually getting worse, and he knew without some type of medical attention the injuries he'd received could become permanent. Unfortunately, he knew that any official hospital visit would result in a call to the police at least, and more likely, a prompt arrest.

He held his side with one hand and wiped tears from his face with the other. He hated this feeling, that the world was unfair. That everything seemed to be hellbent on his downfall. It had been so long since he felt welcomed, and he desperately missed the warmth of human connection. Even his time with Cassius lacked the warmth he felt when speaking to Harper or Sansarev. Perhaps that was why deep down, he felt that Cassius wasn't a real answer for companionship.

"*Sansarev,*" Baxter whispered to himself. It was the last place he could go. The only person he believed had the capacity for forgiveness that he required. He looked down at himself, and through the blurred vision of swollen eyes, he finally had a chance to observe the savage details of his beaten body. He lifted his shirt slightly and assessed his rib cage. The ribs protruded more than he'd ever witnessed before, but then again, he couldn't remember the last time he'd had a decent meal. The definition of his emaciated body also more clearly demonstrated the nature of his wounds from the beating. His ribs no longer held the precise symmetry of the standard frame, but instead, his two central ribs on the left side of his body bent toward one another. The faintest touch of the area caused a sharp blast of pain to shoot through his entire body. The surrounding area had developed numerous different shades of color, and none of the shades remotely resembled the tone of his skin. From the side of his torso began a sickly brown-yellow that melted into a faded gray as it approached the shifted ribs. The faded gray developed into a deeper violet that spread like oil on top of water across the epicenter of the injury. A few short moments of observation was all he could stand before he pulled his shirt back down. Seeing the wound granted no solace from the pain and worsened the hopelessness of his situation.

"Sansarev," he tried to speak with greater volume but found it impossible in anything louder than an unintelligible murmur. He reached up and gently touched his aching jaw, briefly attempting to lift his mandible higher to its original location, but pain once again erupted from the injury.

He thrust his head back in dismay and pressed it against the brick wall behind him. He whimpered and pulled himself back onto his feet. He had a long journey ahead.

"Sansarev."

7

HOMEWARD BOUND

Between relying on backstreets and side roads to avoid the possibility of being identified by a police officer, it took several hours of exhausting discomfort for Baxter to reach his destination. By the time he had arrived, every part of his body was trembling with pain. Looking down a long sloping driveway, he once again set eyes on what he believed was his only hope for salvation, St. Joseph's Orphanage.

Immediately, Baxter's lips began to tremble in a manner unfamiliar to him. The expression felt rigid and alien. He smiled, and it felt awkward. A tear ran down his cheek, and he slowly wiped it away as if reluctant to end the nostalgia. The orphan had returned home.

As he continued to limp down the driveway, he observed a quintet of girls charging through the gardens about twenty meters to his left. They didn't notice the badly wounded vagrant disturbing their picturesque gardens, but instead, giggled at the merriment of their day.

So much has happened in such a relatively short period of time. His journey from St. Joseph's to Hothrest to the streets had aged the boy beyond his years, and with the hard life he'd been living, he felt an uncomfortable disconnect with the jubilant orphans. He, at once, recognized himself as both a returning native and a foreign imposter. The carefree laughter of the girls reminded him of Eliza, and it shocked him how something so innocent and beautiful could instill such anguish and remorse. He recognized his own wretchedness, not just by the terrible events he'd been through, but by the irreparable way they'd changed him. He was glad the girls hadn't seen him. In his current state, he felt he resembled Victor Frankenstein's monster both physically and spiritually. He was a corrupted being of once good intentions that had been twisted by decisions outside of his control. Continuing down the drive, he heard the voices of more children resounding from the back gardens. Each step stirred his memory and imagination in equal doses. As he looked up at each familiar window, he reminisced on who used to live there and wondered how many, if any, of the orphans he knew were still living under Sansarev's wing. He considered what he'd say upon running into Max and Seth again. How much sympathy could he expect from them, if any? He suspected Max would be more welcoming than Seth as they'd spoken at Hothrest, and in general, Max was more liberal with his clemency.

He also thought of Eliza. Ever since leaving St. Joseph's, he'd spent countless hours contemplating what he'd say when they met again and nothing seemed appropriate. At this point, any apology seemed to just redraw old wounds, and any absence of acknowledgement of the past he feared would be perceived as cruel indifference. He paused in front of the entrance and briefly deliberated whether or not returning was a good idea, but as soon as he stepped forward the door swung open, and Sansarev stood speechless in the door frame with an expression of apprehension and disbelief.

"Baxter?" he rasped breathlessly. "Is that you?" he asked taking a few steps forward.

Baxter realized his facial swelling made it nearly impossible for him to be recognized. He attempted a smile at the sight of Sansarev and slowly nodded.

"Oh, my poor boy! Please, come inside. Quickly now!"

The young man briskly followed the old Russian into the foyer of St. Joseph's. He kept his face down to avoid the possibility someone may recognize him as he walked beside the housemaster. Once inside, Sansarev sensed the young man's desire not to be witnessed and motioned for him to head upstairs to the study. Baxter ascended the familiar staircase and turned to head into the Russian's small library. Eventually, Sansarev entered and pulled up a chair beside the boy. He placed his large, rough hand with the greatest tenderness on the young man's swollen jaw and gently moved the mandible while inspecting both sides of Baxter's face. His brow furrowed, and his lips curved into a lamentful frown as he surveyed the damage. His eyes continued upward to the young man's face, and his frown followed. The visage he beheld both saddened and terrified him. In his old ward's face, he saw both the shattered innocence of a child and the trampled hope of an orphan.

"Alejandra will be here shortly with her medical kit," the Russian said softly in an effort to comfort the young man. "My poor poor boy, what happened?"

Baxter reached up and gently touched his horribly swollen face. The concern in his old housemaster's face caused him to notice the pain of the wounds even more than before. "There were a bunch of guys...in Morristown. They cornered me in an alley."

"What were you doing in Morristown? Is that where you went after running from Hothrest?" Sansarev mentioned the asylum without any alteration of his expression. There was no judgement from the Russian, only sincere concern.

"Yeah," Baxter responded, "It was the only place I could think of. I didn't think it would be safe for me to stay anywhere near Hothrest."

"Do you think it's safe for you to be *outside* Hothrest?" returned Sansarev without losing his calm demeanor of compassion.

"I...I honestly don't know." A tear ran down the young man's face as his eyes sank to the floor. "I don't know, but I wasn't getting better. I was getting worse. Much worse."

"How did you escape?" Sansarev asked before quickly interrupting any possible response, "Nevermind. I suppose it's not really important. You came to a place of safety, and that is what you will get." The Russian pulled a wooden pipe from the drawer of his desk and lit it with a long match from his desktop. A ribbon of smoke billowed into the office air, and the aroma of tobacco filled the study. "The gang that did this to you, why?"

"I don't know."

"You don't know why they did this to you?"

"They wanted money," Baxter answered reluctantly.

Sansarev's brow furrowed, and for the better part of a minute, he puffed rings of smoke into the air. "You don't look like the kind of person who would have a significant amount of money. They only wanted money?"

"Or drugs."

"I see. And when you didn't have any, they decided to assault you?"

"Yes."

As Sansarev expelled another rush of smoke from his mouth, Alejandra came in with a bucket of ice and a small satchel marked with a red cross. Her mortification at Baxter's condition was immediately vocalized, "Dios mio, who did this to you!?" she shouted with alarm.

"Alejandra," Sansarev spoke soothingly, "Mr. Bishop's arrival here must not be publicized. Please don't be so loud. I don't want any of the children to know of his presence."

"*And you!*" she growled at the Russian. "You put that

infernal thing away right now, or I'll break it in two!" Sansarev obediently removed the wooden pipe from his mouth, placed it in a decorative tin box, and returned it to the desk drawer from whence it came. "A boy in this condition doesn't need his lungs being filled up with that poisonous gas."

"I hardly think a little smoke is going to do any more significant damage to-" Sansarev's comment was cut short by the dark eyes of Alejandra. They needed no words to silence the Russian, simply their disapproval.

"My dear," Alejandra cooed. Baxter remembered his occasional frustration during his time at St. Joseph's, where he felt coddled for the painful events he'd been through, but his perspective had been changed by the harsh realities of the real world, and he now allowed his eyes to close as he savored the gentle touch of Alejandra's ice pack on his swollen face. "Where else did they hit you?"

"My ribs. I think they're broken."

"Hold this here," she commanded and let go of the ice pack as she carefully began lifting his filthy, torn shirt. As the young man's rib cage became visible, she gasped in shock and turned to Sansarev. "Look at this!"

The housemaster stood from his chair and came to get a closer look at Baxter's torso. "They're certainly in severe disrepair," he said solemnly. "Can you handle this or does he require a hospital?"

"I can't go to a hospital," Baxter quickly reminded his caretakers.

"I understand the situation," Sansarev responded

casually. "There can be complications arising from wounds like this that endanger aspects of your life more important than liberty."

Baxter quieted down, but his face retained a very apprehensive expression.

"Can you manage this?" Sansarev asked Alejandra with his face openly manifesting its own concern.

"I'm not sure. We'll need to keep rotating ice packs on him to keep the swelling down. Once the swelling goes down, we can check on him again to see what isn't healing properly. He shouldn't be walking around like this though. He needs rest."

"Absolutely," agreed the Russian.

Baxter had remained silent for most of Alejandra's examination. The simple experience of being cared for felt simultaneously blissful and foreign. He closed his eyes and felt himself relax for the first time he could remember.

"He can stay here," Sansarev finally declared. "I'll bring in a spare mattress from the attic. It will keep him out of sight of the rest of the children."

"I'll bring his food up before breakfast and after dinner. I'll make sure you have some snacks as well," Alejandra added.

"Thanks," Baxter responded. "It's been a long time since I've had a good meal."

"From the smell of you, it's been a long time since you've had a good bathing, and that's something we'll have to take care of immediately," the Russian quipped, hoping to lighten the situation.

"Do you feel well enough for me to draw a bath," questioned Alejandra.

"I think so. I can smell myself, and I know I need one."

"I'll bring some fresh towels and clothing for you," she continued as she began to depart the room.

"Remember, it's important that you stay in my wing of St. Joseph's, Baxter. The police came here a month or so ago looking for you, and I'd wager they'll come back at some point to double check in case I've heard anything from you. I don't want any of our children telling any of the authorities that there's been a stranger here."

"I understand," Baxter answered with gratitude. "Is anyone I know still here? Seth? Max? Eliza?"

Sansarev thought for a moment before answering, "I'm afraid not. Those three all headed out months ago, maybe even a year. Seth and Max left first. Eliza actually stayed for a few months after all of her friends left. She told me she didn't feel ready to tackle the world outside of St. Joseph's yet."

"Where are they now?" questioned Baxter.

"I'll fill you in on everything soon, Mr. Bishop," the housemaster replied. "For now, I still have an orphanage to run, and you, my friend, need to bathe and rest up. Once you've cleaned yourself up and gotten some rest, I'll come back and get you up to speed on the lives of your colleagues."

"Thank you, Sansarev. For everything."

8

CATCHING UP

Baxter contemplated a shower but quickly decided a bath would be the much less painful choice when it came to washing the dried blood and filth from his body. Alejandra volunteered to help him, explaining she'd already seen everything he had to show, but the young man was adamant about maintaining his privacy.

Although the hot waters of the bath stung his wounds, he still enjoyed the long-forgotten feeling of cleanliness. By the time he'd finished his bath and returned to the study, Sansarev had located a spare mattress and set up a comfortable, little nook in the corner under one of the numerous intimidating bookshelves. Every step Baxter took sent sharp pains throughout his body as some of the more severe cuts had reopened from his bath. He found the clothing that Alejandra had procured for him on the bed and meticulously draped the shirt over his torso. He found raising his arms over his head to be absolutely impossible as the vertical stretching of his rib cage was simply too painful to bear. This required him to contort into unusual positions in order to dress himself with minimal suffering.

Once dressed Baxter carefully positioned himself to slowly fall back onto his bed without bending over and succeeded in achieving a sleeping position without exacerbating any of his wounds. Sansarev came into the study briefly, but as Baxter began to speak, he placed one finger over his lips and hushed the boy. "You need rest, Mr. Bishop. Sleep is your best friend for now." The old Russian departed the study quietly and left the door open a crack just in case Baxter needed to call out for anything.

The pillow felt exceedingly soft underneath Baxter's head, and the constant throbbing from his many swollen contusions finally began to fade. He was happy to be back at St. Joseph's. He was also exhausted.

Baxter didn't dream in the study. Whether it was due to the extent of his exhaustion or some other cause, he was unaware, but his mind was completely dark throughout his slumber. Perhaps the hope that he'd soon be able to rendezvous with Eliza caused his subconscious to vacation from her.

When Baxter awoke, he had no idea the time of day or

how long he'd been out. He felt well rested, but every inch of his body still ached from the beating. Beside the bed he found a small foot stool that either Sansarev or Alejandra had put in place to serve as a makeshift nightstand. On the stool was a glass of water, two small white pills, and a delicate, sterling silver bell. Baxter helped himself to the water but decided to refrain from taking the pills until he was certain of their purpose. He immediately felt childish and distrustful in this decision but rationalized that the cause of his distrust was reasonably derived from the asylum.

Only minutes passed before Sansarev entered. He appeared a bit disheveled, and the area around his eyes suggested he hadn't slept.

"Did you sleep well?" asked the Russian as he reached a hand over his mouth to cover a yawn.

"Yeah. Really well," responded Baxter brightly.

"I'm sure you have a lot of questions, and I wanted to fill you in as soon as you felt ready."

"Thanks. You said everyone had left..."

Sansarev chuckled, "Well not *everyone*. St. Joseph's always has a fresh rotation of youngsters coming through its doors, but yes, your friends, Eliza, Max, and Seth, have all departed for the real world."

"You said Eliza didn't feel ready at first?"

"Yes. Eliza's recovery was slow. She spent most of her time away from the other children. She'd stay in her room for long hours reading, writing, drawing, or whatever would distract her. I imagine that's something the two of you ended up having in common."

Baxter looked up, "What's that?"

"You both became rather consumed with memories and nightmares about the tragedies you'd been through. Where you worked with Dr. Schaffer to overcome your nightmares, Eliza used various artistic pursuits to ease her pain. You know, writing, painting, and the like."

"Where is she now?" the young man questioned slowly, uncertain as to whether the information was appropriate to share.

"St. Joseph's works with charitable members of the community to help establish modest homes for our children who aren't adopted by the time they reach adulthood. Although I rarely visit these homes, I believe Eliza has a small apartment in town. The actual address I'm afraid I don't know."

"Seth and Max?"

"Essentially the same situation for Max. Seth took an apprenticeship with a carpenter and has left the area. I'm not sure where he is now as I believe the carpenter who he's working with travels a great deal." Sansarev picked up one of his baubles from a bookshelf and began dexterously manipulating the object with his right hand as he always did when preparing to initiate an awkward conversation.

Sansarev shuffled through his desk and pulled out a neatly folded newspaper before sitting down in a chair beside Baxter's cot. "This came out a couple of months ago, and although we had no idea where you were, I hoped I'd see you again, and if you didn't already know, I figured you'd want to read it." He handed the paper to Baxter and gestured for the young man to read.

Baxter apprehensively began reading the article Sansarev had circled in black:

> *Late last night law enforcement officers arrested Mr. Patrick Fenway in downtown Morristown. Fenway was placed in custody after a police investigation ascertained that he may have been involved in the orchestrated killing of a married couple in a quiet suburb three years ago. Fenway worked as a prominent attorney in Morristown. No information has been released to the public as to the state's case or motives for his involvement.*

Baxter's mouth remained open halfway through the article and continued to be open after he'd finished reading. "Was this my home?" he asked.

Sansarev nodded.

"When did this happen?"

"The paper is from about a month ago. I've been in touch with Detective Caine over at the station, but he said there've been no developments in the case since the article. Apparently, they picked him up in Morristown for the murder of your parents, but he's, unsurprisingly, intending to plead not guilty and pointing the finger at Dr. Schaffer. Caine informed me between the testimony of the man in custody and discovered correspondence, they now have proof that your father..." At this point, Sansarev abruptly stopped speaking and reached his right hand up to pensively stroke his thick beard.

"What about my father?" Baxter prodded.

The housemaster didn't answer immediately, but instead, continued to gently stroke his beard while displaying a stern, thoughtful countenance. After a few moments of methodical contemplation, he continued, "According to Detective Caine, given the uncovered correspondence, they have evidence that your father and Dr. Schaffer were involved in a romantic affair for some time before your parents' death."

"A romantic affair...?" For the first time in over a day, the physical pain that covered Baxter's body was replaced with the familiar, acidic stone that dropped to the bottom of his stomach. "My father was having sex with Dr. Schaffer?"

"That is what they believe, yes."

"Before he was killed?"

"Yes."

"Why was he killed?"

"I don't think they'll ever know for certain unless they find Dr. Schaffer. Until then, it's all just the story of an accused murderer at this point. Since Schaffer has vanished, it's going to be difficult to get the whole story."

"But Schaffer had something to do with it?"

"I don't know, Baxter. They don't know either. They believe so, but without any other information on Schaffer, there's no way to be certain or to discover more. The case isn't closed by any means, but it's been a dead end in terms

of prosecution at the moment. They have romantic correspondence between Schaffer and your father, and they'll
probably hold off on Fenway's trial for as long as possible
in hopes that the the good doctor turns up. If Schaffer
returns to the area, she'll definitely be brought into the
station for interrogation, but I don't see her coming back
here if she did have anything to do with this."

"Who the fuck is Patrick Fenway? Why would he do
this?"

Every time such coarse language exited the young man's
mouth, Sansarev winced, but he understood the emotional
turmoil that was churning deep inside Baxter. The idea
that an adult, and more accurately, a mentor, had been
an agent in the murder of the young man's parents was a
blood-boiling concept for even the old Russian to contem-
plate. "I don't have the slightest idea. Caine showed me a
picture of Fenway. He appeared to be an upright citizen.
Why anyone wanted your parents dead? I have no idea;
especially given that Dr. Schaffer may have had feelings for
your father. I suppose that's where we stand. We have stories of what happened, but no idea why. No clear motive."

Baxter fell back down onto the cot and held his hands
over his face. Every time he felt closure was close by, it
would sleep through his fingers like sand, leaving him
with an emotional solution of equal parts sorrow and
frustration.

"Baxter?" Sansarev spoke softly.

"Yes?" the young man answered as he pulled his hands
away from his face.

"I don't care that you ran from Hothrest."

"Thank you," Baxter let out a deep breath. "It's relieving to know that. I had to leave, but I wasn't sure how you'd feel about it."

"Your flight from the asylum doesn't concern me, but I want to know what you've been doing these past three months. You show up at St. Joseph's nearly beaten to death and claiming that a gang jumped you looking for money or drugs in an alleyway. I don't know if you remember, but I lived on the streets once. I know what vices are out there, and I know the types of questions young men in desperate times ask. I know what answers they seek, and I know the mistakes they make while seeking comfort."

Baxter remained silent but kept his gaze fixed on Sansarev.

"Are you clean, Mr. Bishop?"

"Clean?"

"Drugs, Baxter. Are you currently taking any drugs? I know they had you on some serious medications at the asylum. It couldn't have been easy to cut those out of your life so quickly."

"I stopped taking the drugs at Hothrest. I kept them in my cheek until the nurses and orderlies left then I'd spit them out and hide them in a wad of gum under my bed. I rarely took the drugs they gave me."

"So you're clean then; you haven't been doing them on the streets?" questioned Sansarev again.

Baxter felt apprehensive with Sansarev's repeated question as if he somehow already knew. The Russian had forgiven much worse from the young man, and he didn't wish to begin lying to his old housemaster at this point. "After I ran away from Hothrest, I lived under a bridge outside Morristown for a few months. I wanted to stay out of sight because I knew if the police found me, I'd go to prison, not Hothrest. Although, I think at this point, I'd prefer that." Baxter cleared his throat. He intended to tell Sansarev everything, but he still felt a terrible gnawing guilt at what he feared would disappoint his dear friend. "I used to search for food in the alleys and dumpsters outside restaurants. It was filthy and disgusting, but I had to survive. About a week ago, I ran into a guy a little bit older than me. He invited me to his place. He was alone as well, and his apartment was pretty much just an abandoned closet in another alley. His name was Scott, but he said his friends called him Stretch so that's what I called him. Once while I was staying at Stretch's place, he gave me a pipe with drugs, and I did it once - there - with him. I've never done it since." At the end of his story, he exhaled sharply. He was still worried about Sansarev's response but felt relieved about getting the weight off his chest.

Sansarev returned to quietly brushing his beard with his hand. "Thank you for being honest with me, Baxter. I'm not angry at in you for doing what you've done. Sometimes things can get so dark, we'll do anything to try and find a light, but this is your first and last warning. If I find even a trace of drugs in this orphanage, I will drive you to the county jail myself. Do you understand?"

"Yes."

"I do not endanger the children of St. Joseph's. Do you understand that?"

"Yes, sir," Baxter responded solemnly.

"If you stay here, it is on the condition that you will no longer use *any* drugs."

"Yes, sir."

"Good." Sansarev finally smiled, and a subtle trace of color returned to his complexion. "For both of our safety, you should stay in my wing of the orphanage until the children have gone to bed. There's more windows in my bedroom, and you're more than welcome to spend time during the day in there as well. Don't want you wasting away in the shadows!" The housemaster chuckled while gently tugging at his beard.

"Thank you, Sansarev."

"You know. It's just that if word got out to the authorities in any way, we'd both be in quite a sticky spot."

"I understand," responded the young man obediently.

"Good. Now then, is there anything I can help you with? I need to get down and help Alejandra with the barbarian hordes." The Russian smiled, "No matter how long I look after these kids, they never seem to make any more sense to me. They are unapologetic Huns! Every one!"

Baxter watched from his bed as Sansarev left. Besides the constant throbbing of his entire body, he felt good to be back at the orphanage. He appreciated the stern but caring eye of Sansarev and was happy to return to his teenage sanctuary.

9

ANSWERED QUESTIONS OR QUESTIONED ANSWERS?

The rest of the day for Baxter was a combination of calm born from his return to St. Joseph's and anger at the revelation that Schaffer had been an agent in his original trauma. All the memories of appointments with his old therapist haunted him while he lay prostrate on his firm cot in the orphanage study. All the advice she'd given, and all the therapy she'd provided caused Baxter's stomach to turn. He felt not only betrayed but like a traitor himself. Every moment he could recall with her left him gritting his teeth in a quiet brooding rage, but even with these recent developments from Sansarev, hard questions still tickled the back of the young man's mind. Was he selected because of his parents or were they selected because of him? It was a simple conclusion to reach that all the coincidences within these events couldn't be so simple. There had to be more to the story, but how he'd ever know without Schaffer remained a conundrum.

Time passed in the study with the contemplation of these unknown variables. Occasionally, the pain from his wounds would demand his attention, but quickly after, his mind would return to his parents and Schaffer. He partially blamed himself for not learning more from Schaffer when he'd suspected her dishonesty, but the opportunity to discover more seemed to have passed.

Sansarev returned to the study later that evening after making sure his wards had been fed and were prepared to retire to their bedrooms when the time came. He swiftly sat down next to the cot and returned without hesitation to their previous discussion concerning his parents' case. "About a month after you escaped Hothrest, Detective Caine and Dr. Brent came by St. Joseph's in hopes I'd have some information on your whereabouts. As you had not articulated your plans to me, I was completely in the dark as to where you could have gone. They both left, but on the way out, Detective Caine asked me if I'd keep him in the loop, should you turn up. This was purposefully mentioned out of earshot of Dr. Brent, and I believe Caine may be interested in talking with you." The Russian cleared his throat and scratched his head, "I don't know the man well enough to make a decision for you, and I know there's the possibility he would just take you into custody, but I got the feelin' that this meeting would be of a clandestine nature."

Baxter exhaled sharply and spoke slowly as he weighed the prospect of meeting Caine. "I want to do whatever I can to help. Do you really think he won't take me to jail?"

"I honestly don't have any idea," responded Sansarev shrugging. "If you'd like, I can call him in an attempt to get a better understanding of his intentions. He seemed only concerned about your whereabouts in terms of how you could potentially help his case."

"I'd appreciate you doing that," replied Baxter. "I think I can trust him, but I'd like to know more. I can't go back to jail...or Hothrest."

"I'm not convinced either of those places are beneficial for you. I'll phone Detective Caine, but you still need to get some rest. I imagine if he sees you with all those cuts and bruises, he'll be more inclined to place you back in an institution."

"What better place than an orphanage?" joked Baxter.

"If I thought there was a better place to serve, I'd be serving there," responded the Russian. "I'll call Caine this afternoon, and we can discuss our next steps once I know more. But for now, you get some rest."

"Thanks," Baxter offered as Sansarev turned and exited. The housemaster didn't respond with words. He simply knocked on the solid wood door frame as he left the study.

Baxter's injuries from the beating were healing slowly so the opportunity to recuperate in a quiet place was a treasured situation. Sansarev returned just before midnight with Alejandra's leftovers from dinner. He entered quietly, but once he saw Baxter awake, he began whistling as he tidied up around the young man's bed.

"How's everything been going?" Baxter asked as he turned over to his side. He urgently wanted to know what had come from the conversation with Caine, but he felt it would be rude to immediately jump to his desired topic. He moved slowly in order to mitigate the inevitable pain from his rib cage.

Seeing his grimace, Sansarev came over and sat on the edge of the bed. "Don't move too much before we have a chance to better evaluate the extent of the damage. Alejandra told me she's afraid your ribs may have punctured another organ when they shifted. I hope she's wrong, but with your entire torso being discolored, I think we should play it safe."

"I understand," the young man agreed.

"Everything's goin' well around here, I suppose," Sansarev said returning to the previously unanswered question. "None of our children have been made aware of your presence, and I intend to keep it that way. Once your recovery is complete, we can discuss other options. It certainly doesn't make any sense for you to spend the rest of your life in my study."

Baxter let out a short laugh, "I know. This was the only place I felt safe."

"I know."

"Once I can, I'll leave town. I don't know where I'll go or what I'll do, but I know there's no real life for me here."

Sansarev paused for a moment as he brooded over the orphan's dilemma. He didn't deny the truth behind Baxter's pain, but he did tense up at what he perceived as his own shortcomings failing the young man. "It gives me no pleasure to say this, Mr. Bishop, but an orphanage is no home for an adult, trust me, I know. I've been homeless for longer than I can remember. The key is to find a place and make it your home. I know one day you will leave, and I know it will be best for you if you leave this area, but I doubt you'll have any trouble making wherever you land your home."

"None of the places I've been were homes except here."

"This *was* your home, but it can't be anymore. You're grown, and this isn't a home for a grown man. Not to mention if word ever got out that you'd returned to the area, I'm certain St. Joseph's is the first place the authorities would search."

"I know," Baxter responded with reluctance. "I came back because it's the only place I have. The entire time I knew in the back of my mind that I couldn't stay."

"One day you'll find a better place than this, a place more appropriate for you, a place more accommodating for your needs."

"I think I'm done acting on desires. They've got me nothing but problems," the young man joked with a wry smile.

Sansarev let out hearty chuckle, "No man is finished acting on his desires. That's our nature. With our best attempts, we can only hope to minimize the damage." Sansarev briefly glanced out the door into the hall before continuing with a mischievous smile on his face, "Hedonism is like a beautiful woman. She'll make everything seem like heaven tonight, but she'll hurt you tomorrow."

"Making sure Alejandra isn't in earshot?" Baxter laughed.

"Always," responded the Russian playfully. "But also I wanted to speak with you about my promised conversation with Detective Caine. I didn't mention your presence here, but I did prod him for a better understanding of their position on the case of your parents. It appears quite a bit has been uncovered through the criminal grapevine concerning what happened that evening."

"So you didn't tell him I was here?"

"I did not. It never seemed to be necessary."

"What did he say?" the young man queried with an excited whisper.

"His department brought in Fenway after an informant overheard he had offered money for..." Sansarev paused as he always did when discussing the grizzly details of that night. "Apparently he was offering to pay someone to harm your parents. They don't seem to have any more information as to who he paid or what exactly the motive was for the crime."

"Nothing was taken," the young man said, seeking to remind the Russian.

"That's true, and I'm afraid it leads to the target likely being your parents."

"Maybe Schaffer was angry at my father for something. Or she could've been jealous of my mother," the young man responded, trying to develop his thoughts concerning the crime.

Sansarev opened his mouth to caution the young man on jumping to conclusions but was immediately cut off by Alejandra loudly whispering from the stairwell. "Sergei! Telephone!" she called urgently.

The late hour of Alejandra's interruption caused Sansarev to give the young man a curious look before excusing himself and departing the study. Baxter sat alone on his cot, contemplating all the new information he'd been recently given, but unable to make heads or tails of all the seemingly disjointed evidence. He was certain Schaffer was involved in some nefarious manner, but given his outlaw status, he felt helpless in pursuing the truth.

No more than a few moments had passed before Sansarev slowly reappeared in the doorway with an astounded expression. He shook his head in a dazed manner before speaking slowly, sounding as though he didn't completely believe his own words. "That was Detective Caine." He paused again, searching for the correct way to say something that must certainly be incorrect. "The police have Dr. Schaffer in custody."

10

CROSSROADS

Baxter leapt from the cot with such vigor that his body immediately writhed in pain and sent him falling back down onto the makeshift bed. "She was arrested?" he questioned with an incredulous tone.

"Apparently, she went downtown to speak to the police."

"So she was responsible?"

"In some way, possibly," the housemaster answered each question in an uncertain manner, half due to his shock at the event, half due to his ignorance of legal procedure, which he was entirely self-aware. "Caine asked that I drop by the station sometime tomorrow to speak with him about my interactions with her, and the interactions between the two of you that I witnessed. Is there anything you haven't told me about your sessions that you'd like to before I speak to him?"

Baxter paused for a moment in contemplation but

couldn't immediately recall any event that held any relevance to the ongoing situation. "I don't believe so," he responded slowly, "But if I think of anything I'll definitely let you know. I can't believe it.

Sansarev let out a deep breath as he rubbed his eyes that were now clearly encouraging him to retire for the night. The hour was late, and he knew tomorrow was going to be another long day wrought with emotion. "You're not going to be able to sleep tonight, are you?"

"I doubt it," responded Baxter with nervous enthusiasm. "I feel like every piece of the puzzle will be explained tomorrow. I'm too anxious to sleep."

"That may be, but I wouldn't get your hopes too high. We don't really have that much information about what they know or what she's said. I'd be shocked if whatever happens tomorrow answers all your questions."

"I know you're right, but it's still exciting to have any of them answered. I feel like I've been left out of the loop for such a long time." The boy's feet were frantically tapping against the floor in a display of unconcealable excitement.

"Well, I'm completely exhausted," chuckled Sansarev. "If you don't mind, I'll be leaving you for the night. As much as I hope this answers all the questions we may have, I still have an orphanage to run, and I've been running on fumes the last couple of days."

"I understand," responded Baxter. "Thank you."

"Try to get some sleep if you can. We'll have much to talk about tomorrow. Obviously, we'll discuss what I learn tomorrow from Caine; however, we'll also want to discuss your future."

"Thanks," the orphan repeated gratefully as he slid his legs back under the covers and lay his head on the soft pillow.

Upon awakening, Baxter felt an immediate sense of surprise that he'd actually been able to fall asleep. All the excitement from the previous night and the epiphanies it held excited the young man. So many questions he'd desperately needed answered were all finally starting to become clearer in his mind. Unfortunately, he'd have to wait until Sansarev returned from his meeting with Caine before he could uncover the deeper truths. Alejandra had left food on the nearby desk at some point in the morning, but the young man lacked any appetite. He poked his head into Sansarev's quarters, but the housemaster had already left his chambers. He knew he was forbidden from entering the rest of St. Joseph's so he returned to the study and sat sullenly in Sansarev's chair, staring with disinterest at the lukewarm breakfast in front of him.

"Looks like some stuff is coming together for ya," commented Cassius. Baxter hadn't noticed him perusing one of Sansarev's bookcases until he spoke.

"Can you believe all this? My dad and Schaffer?"

"Schaffer's a good looking girl. Not too shocking," chuckled the older man.

"Funny," responded Baxter, clearly not amused by the joke.

"I'd check your excitement, kid," returned Cassius. "If Schaffer went to the station, there's something she wants to say. There's a big part of this we don't know anything about yet."

"It's a smaller piece than yesterday," Baxter reminded his friend with a look of accomplishment.

"We've been at this long enough, man. You're gonna have more questions. This isn't gonna wrap everything up in a nice tidy package for ya. It just ain't gonna happen." Cassius tossed a couple rebellious dreads out of his face. "There's only one way to get to the *real* bottom."

"Oh yeah, and what do you suggest?"

"Ya gotta dig, kid. Yourself."

"What do you mean?" questioned Baxter.

"You said it yourself. You can't stay here. That old Russian knows it too. You have to move on. *Ya not a little orphan boy anymo'*", he mocked in a baby-voice, "Your whole life you've just done what others told you. Where has it gotten you? Shit, if it wasn't for me, you'd still be in Hothrest choking down pills in a strait-jacket while Brent yakked himself to death."

"I can leave here when I'm better and find out what I need to. Doesn't mean I'm not going to learn more when Sansarev returns."

"Meh, I guess we'll see," Cassius returned indifferently. "You can't tell me you think either this Fenway guy or Schaffer is gonna tell the truth. It's murder. There's no plea here that keeps them out of prison. Schaffer isn't putting cuffs on herself. She'll walk in and out of that station today. I promise ya that much."

Baxter became aggravated at the realization that Cassius was bringing up salient points. He flopped back down on his cot with a loud, exasperated sigh. He lay still, desperately attempting to untie the many knots that existed in his head. *What role did Schaffer have? Could he have done anything to stop it? What about Fenway?*

Upon hearing footsteps coming from the stairwell, Baxter rose with enthusiasm from the cot and inconspicuously poked his head around the door frame to catch a glimpse of his potential visitor. When Sansarev's figure appeared, he quickly spun back into the office and waited with anticipation. As the Russian turned the corner into the study, he chuckled at the young man standing at attention, ready for his arrival.

"Hello there, Mr. Bishop! It's great to see you out of bed and looking ready to tackle the day," he joked.

Baxter smiled at Sansarev's playful avoidance of the obvious topic of interest. "Yeah, I'm great. So?" he laughed.

"My sweet boy, we have so much to discuss."

11

REVELATIONS

Sansarev left the study to make certain Alejandra wasn't in the wing before he returned and quietly pulled his pipe out of his desk. He smiled at Baxter, "I know she'd kill me if she caught me enjoying my pipe around you, but this is my only sanctuary in this orphanage so I hope you don't mind if I partake."

"Of course not, just tell me what you found out!" Baxter exclaimed in a loud, anxious whisper. "Did you see Schaffer?"

The Russian puffed on his pipe a few times before responding, "Yes, I saw Schaffer. I didn't get to speak with her, but Caine informed me of both her and Fenway's stories. Sadly, it ends up that there was quite a twisted triangle of misplaced intimacy. Schaffer and Fenway's relationship was also romantically inclined it seems."

"The man that murdered my parents was also sleeping with Schaffer?" Baxter spoke with his jaw open in astoundment. "She had to be involved then!"

"It's difficult to believe she wasn't, but that's why she claimed to have been at the station: to clear her name in a highly suspect scenario."

"What reason would Fenway have to harm my parents?"

"According to the informant, apparently he went to your house to...confront your father....you should know that Schaffer and Fenway's stories don't totally match up."

"But what about my mother, and how are their stories different?" Baxter prodded nervously, frightened of the answers to his questions.

"Given the intimate nature of these relationships, I'm not sure if anyone even knew your mother existed. She may have been a completely innocent party in this entire thing. Fenway claims he had nothing to do with it. Schaffer claims complete ignorance, but she's still not speaking freely to authorities. She came to the station with an attorney in toe, and according to Caine, was extremely cautious with the questions she was allowed to answer and the details provided."

"What did Detective Caine say?"

"He said he's never seen anything like it. Schaffer's not being as cooperative with the investigation as you'd expect from an innocent party. Caine told me he wasn't at liberty to discuss some things, but there were pieces of evidence that point at Schaffer absolutely being involved. I'm sorry, Mr. Bishop. It's a twisted and hazy situation down there."

"What evidence?"

"Caine couldn't tell me. He said it was a highly confidential investigation, and he wasn't at liberty to discuss those details. He did mention that Fenway's connections as an attorney in Morristown would almost certainly complicate matters. He has friends on the force and in the courts. I believe that's one of the reasons the investigation is being kept so close to the chest for law enforcement."

Baxter's brow furrowed in thought as he tried to recall any information from his own history that could help illuminate any part of the case. He frowned when he found himself just as bewildered as he'd been before Sansarev's briefing. "So they think Fenway did it, but he's claiming he didn't. There may be evidence that points to Schaffer, and she's not really cooperating?" He sighed with exasperation, "I suppose I was naive to hope for a simple answer after all this time."

"Hope is usually as naive as it is necessary," responded Sansarev. "I'm sorry to bring this up, but there is some bad news."

Baxter didn't speak but responded to the Russian with a dejected look.

"It ends up you were recognized during your encounter downtown last week. Caine informed me that the officer you ran from identified you as Baxter Bishop, and the department has restarted its manhunt for you."

Baxter's voice was mixed with fear and uncertainty as he replied, "But I didn't do anything wrong. I was attacked by that gang."

"I believe you, but you don't have the luxury of protection under the law. You signed away your safety when you fled Hothrest. The police aren't going to care in the slightest about crimes committed against you. You're one of *them* now."

"One of *them?*"

"You're a criminal, Mr. Bishop."

Baxter became silent, and a profound sadness overwhelmed him. He felt a deep sense of inner turmoil about the label that Sansarev had so casually bestowed upon him, but he immediately recognized the obvious and bold accuracy of the title.

Cassius began quietly cackling in the corner of the room like a loquacious raven, "You didn't realize you were a criminal? I'm sorry, kid, but that is a little funny."

Baxter's head turned slightly as he processed Cassius' comment, but he clearly didn't share his companion's amusement concerning this realization. "They want me as bad as they want whoever killed my parents." It chilled the orphan to acknowledge the company he was with from a legal perspective. It was the first time he'd been grouped with the people who had taken everything from him, and comprehending this left the young man feeling bitterly alienated. "It's not fair," he muttered.

"Fair?" laughed Cassius as he thumbed through a book from the shelves.

"The world rarely is, Mr. Bishop," commented Sansarev. "But we shouldn't perseverate on such inequities. The cut worm forgives the plow."

"What? The worm forgives the plow?" Baxter returned puzzled.

"William Blake," the Russian answered. "It means we must accept the nature of things."

"I don't deserve this."

"The fox condemns the trap, not himself."

Baxter sighed with exasperation, "More Blake?"

Sansarev smiled, "Yes."

"Ugh, whatever," Baxter murmured. "How are they so sure it was me? My eyes were swollen shut. How could they recognize me?"

"I'm not sure, Baxter. I didn't speak to anyone except Caine. They have multiple witnesses identifying you as in terrible shape and in need of immediate medical assistance. I imagine they'll begin their sweep where they last lost you, but unfortunately, I'm certain they'll be here at some point. I wish I could take care of you until you were fully healed, but-"

"You're in danger the longer I'm here. I understand that. If I'm found here, they'd never believe you weren't responsible for hiding me. I won't put you in danger."

"Where would you go if you left St. Joseph's?" Sansarev questioned.

"Back on the streets," Baxter responded with uncertainty. He expected Sansarev to object. "I don't know," he offered as a vague compromise.

"Do you think it's a safe idea for you to just simply leave?"

"No, but I don't know what else to do."

The old Russian's hand returned to the familiar territory of his beard while he deliberated on the conundrum. Deep down, he felt terrified at the idea of leaving Baxter alone on the streets again, but he knew he couldn't let that terror keep him from doing what was best for the rest of the children under his care. If Baxter was discovered at St. Joseph's, Sansarev knew he'd be held culpable for harboring the boy. They would hopefully be lenient on the housemaster given the relationship between the two, but he wasn't certain how far that mercy would extend, and he wasn't willing to jeopardize the welfare of the orphanage. "You should rest here until tomorrow, at least. They won't be coming here immediately, and we could use the time to prepare you for your departure. You can eat well today, sleep well tonight, and tomorrow we can decide on the best course of action. Does that sound reasonable?" Sansarev was clearly vexed, but he'd come up with what he felt was a satisfactory decision.

"Yeah, thank you, Sansarev," the orphan responded meekly. He immediately felt exhausted, as though all of the emotional turmoil of the day had crashed down on him suddenly. Sansarev recognized the boy's wilting demeanor and excused himself to attend to the various chores that needed completion around the orphanage. He had a long list of tasks that needed completing before he sent his wayward child back into the storm.

12

SONNY, MOVE OUT TO THE COUNTRY

Baxter curled up on his cot and reminded himself to enjoy the comforting warmth and softness of the fresh sheets. They were one of the small things he'd come to relish at the orphanage, knowing that once he went back to the streets, there'd be no such amenities to comfort the body or mind. He didn't feel as scared or discouraged as he'd expected by the discovery that he'd have to return to his previous homelessness. His wounds were still sore, and any sudden movements still caused his body to ache, but the last few days had been heavensent for the young man's recovery. His convalescence at the nurturing hands of Alejandra had been a boon for his badly damage body as well as his emotional state. Being around people that seemed to genuinely care about his well being was what he'd miss the most when he returned to the streets. He recalled the loneliness of his orientation at St. Joseph's without his parents. He recalled the first days at Hothrest without Sansarev and his fellow orphans. He remembered sitting under his bridge outside Morristown, throwing rocks into the small stream that slithered through the camp, and how he'd missed Nurse Harper. He chuckled to himself at even missing Dr. Brent.

"They shouldn't call it homelessness," joked Cassius, "They should call it carelessness. You end up not caring about anything because there isn't anything caring about you. It'd help all the princes and princesses with their perfect lives to understand what it really is."

"At least it's warmer this time of year," Baxter offered.

"And it's going to keep getting warmer until it's hot," Cassius countered, "The comfortable season ends one way or another."

"We'll be free."

Cassius chuckled and began singing, *"Freedom, well that's just some people talkin', your prison is walking through the world all alo-."*

"Don't be so depressing. We've been through worse," Baxter interrupted with an annoyed tone.

"Is that what we're holding onto now? That we've been through worse? So proud of you! The kid who's been in and out of, let's see, an orphanage, a prison, an asylum ... but we're doing great now because we're about to be *just homeless.*"

"You don't have to come if you don't want to," Baxter smiled sheepishly.

Cassius let out a loud laugh and clapped his hands

together, "Alright, kid, you win; you win! So what's the plan?"

"The plan for what?"

"The plan for us; the plan for Schaffer and that Fenway guy."

"I don't think there's anything I can do about that situation right now. I suppose we just have to wait and see what Detective Caine finds out. They won't get away with it; I promise you that. I don't care who they are; they'll answer for what they did," Baxter seethed, gritting his teeth in anger.

"I'm going to get some rest while I have a bed to rest in. Tomorrow morning we'll talk to Sansarev and find out what the plan is."

Baxter tightly wrapped the sheets around his body and allowed his mind to zone out, attempting to only focus on the comforting effect of the linens. He slowed his breathing and rubbed his head against the clean pillow. Tonight would be his last evening in comfort, and he decided to take full advantage of it. It wasn't long before his eyes became heavy, and he peacefully fell asleep for the last time at St. Joseph's.

13

GREAT BALLS OF FIRE

As the dream began, Baxter felt enthused at how fluidly his mind recognized the fantasy; however, his enthusiasm quickly waned when he realized the event that his subconscious had chosen to project. It was the last night he spent with his parents; the night of their death, and although registering this immediately put the dreamer on edge, he committed himself to courage with the reassurance that he was in complete control. To demonstrate his control, he looked down at his hand, focused his mind, and spoke, "Fire." Before he finished the syllable, a small flame appeared in the palm of his hand and illuminated the dark bedroom. A wide smile spread across Baxter's face as he admired his proficiency with dream-governance, and immediately upon recognizing this blossoming strength, he turned his head with conviction toward the old staircase that he knew descended into his nightmare. His last recollection of this place was from horrific nightmares during his year at Hothrest. The memories filled the dreamer with apprehension, but he returned his gaze to the fire he had created, and with a focused glare, caused the flame to burn brighter until the entire staircase was bathed in a supernatural glow. Witnessing his new power caused Baxter's confidence to surge, and he playfully juggled the flame from hand to hand like a tennis ball. The young man began his descent with a feeling of total impunity; his imagination weaponized and limitless. The previous memories of trepidation dissolved in his newfound strength, and he marvelled at the flame as it flickered menacingly in the palms of his hands. As he took the final step from the stairs, his foot fell into a shallow pool of water that spread across the floor. Baxter remembered this environment from his previous dream and smiled at his recollection. The feeling of familiarity, and the knowledge of what power that familiarity could produce, was immensely satisfying. He knelt in the water and placed one of his flaming palms flat against the flooded, wood floor. The fire was instantly extinguished in the pool. Baxter bent lower until his lips were nearly touching the clear surface and whispered, "Flow."

No sooner had the words left the dreamer's mouth then the water began rapidly rushing away from the hand toward the exits and out of the room. The cascading water rushed against the walls of the home, and the many small tributaries that formed in the various rooms eventually came together to form a massive wave that surged down the main hallway with incredible velocity and gushed out the open back door. Baxter rose from his kneeling position and laughed as he reignited the fire and happily juggled it in the air like a tennis ball. As the ball passed between his hands for the third time, he heard a shattering crash from his parents' room. He'd been so busy admiring his ability to govern the dream that he'd completely forgotten what would likely be happening down the hall. The thought of entering his parents' bed chamber was the first thing in the dreamscape that caused Baxter to hesitate. Was he stable enough to handle the emotional impact of what he might see? Would he be able to maintain his control over the dream or would he slip into nightmare? These questions riddled the young man as he gathered his courage and continued down the long corridor to the door that rested, as he remembered it, slightly ajar.

As he placed his right hand on the bedroom door, he fought back fear and tried to remain stalwart in the face of what had been the most horrifying moment of his life. With his left hand, he formed a fist, and the fire that had once resided in his palm now overtook the rest of his hand, turning his fist into a torch. The door opened easily, and the dreamer looked out onto the scene he remembered. He chose not to govern or manipulate the scene. He wanted his memories intact in case there was anything that could aid his pursuit of justice. He grit his teeth and held back his emotions as everything he remembered came into view. His mother lay on the floor beside the broken glass and the puddle of blood that leaked from her inanimate body. Her eyes caused the most anxiety within the dreamer. They seemed to cry out for help as an expression of total horror occupied them. Baxter took a deep breath and imagined the events he had just witnessed.

She lay awake, happily reading a romance novel beside her husband. The evening seemed like any other night, pleasant in its banality. As she casually turned the page, she heard the shuffling of feet from outside and paused her reading to pay closer attention. Her husband, whose nightly peace had also been interrupted by the unusual sounds, sat up and contemplated whether or not he should venture outside and investigate the disturbance. She alleviated his concern with a gentle hand to his shoulders. "It's probably just a racoon or a possum," she offered in a hushed tone.

"Yeah, you're probably right," the man answered. "I tied the lids down on the cans, so he's shit out of luck if he thinks he's getting into the garb-"

Before he could finish his thought, a body flew through the window and jagged shards showered the room. The broken glass exploded in slow motion for the dreamer and spilled onto the nightstand, the bed, and the floor, leaving an entrancing, explosion of shards that reflected the lamp light from the overturned nightstand.

There was no time to react to the unpredictable event. She screamed, and the scream immediately felt familiar to Baxter. It was the same unrehearsed cry that had awoken him several years ago. He felt his heart race, but he focused on remaining calm to keep the dreamscape stable.

For a brief moment, the faceless adversary gathered its senses from crashing through the window and slowly rose, surrounded by a malevolent aura. The being had no face but was clothed in filthy, baggy garments that concealed any possible details of its figure. It stood and silently stared into the eyes of Baxter before turning its attention back to his mother and father. His mother was pressed against the headboard, clutching the sheets and comforter close to her bosom. His father was frozen with his mouth agape, unable to process the unfathomable and terrifying occurence. The intruder brandished a large knife at the couple and lunged with shocking speed across the bed. The intruder landed on Baxter's father and stabbed the blade down into the comforter that was covering his torso. His father cried out in pain and threw his arms around the figure in an attempt to wrestle the weapon out of the being's hands, but the intruder held onto the blade with an uncompromising grip. The blade rose and fell again into the flesh of Baxter's father, and he shouted out in pain as the vagrant tore the blade back out of his body. His father looked up into the featureless face of the being with a look of bewilderment and fear as the blood quickly evacuated his body from the two deep lacerations.

Baxter shook with rage as the scene continued. He desperately wished to intervene and unleash his wrath on the imposter, but he knew his interference would end the event, and he hoped there was more he could learn from experiencing the tragedy so vividly. He resolved to grit his teeth and suffer the violence.

The being rose from his father's body and turned its attention to his mother who had fallen from the bed onto the floor below. As the being began crawling off the bed to assault its next victim, Baxter's father reached out with his fading strength to grab onto the arm of the figure, but his strength failed him, and the adversary easily knocked his hand away and threw the comforter over his father's face. Baxter's mother attempted to flee from the room, but the intruder leapt from the mattress and tackled her into the bedroom wall. The two fell with a thud, but the being quickly wrestled her to the ground, straddled her flailing body, and waved the blade menacingly an inch from her lips. The intruer's face, which was almost entirely feature-less, turned only partially towards Baxter and displayed a wicked smile. At this point, the rage was too much for the young man to withhold, and as he felt his muscles tighten, he glanced down at the weakly flickering flame still meekly holding onto life in his left hand.

The impostor placed the point of its blade to his moth-er's stomach and slowly began pushing the dagger into her flesh.

"NO!" Baxter erupted and tackled the being from his mother's body. The two rolled over the broken glass and collided into the upturned bedside table. The being slashed the blade at Baxter's face, but the young man leaned away and watched as the blade passed harmlessly past his nose. He jumped up from the ground and positioned himself

between his mother and the being, raising his left hand and encouraging the flame to strengthen. The fire obeyed the dreamer instantly and burst into a massive blaze. The being slashed its knife two more times towards the boy, but it quickly recognized its weaponry was outmatched and began searching for a means of escape. Baxter recognized the being's intentions and reach out his left hand towards his opponent. He commanded the flame, "Burn."

As the word left his mouth, the fire heeded his command. It lunged as if from a flamethrower and swiftly surrounded the being, enveloping the figure in an intense conflagration. The being hissed and shrieked as it awkwardly writhed against the wall in agony. Baxter admired his handiwork, and for a brief moment, smiled at the destruction he'd caused to the being, but the feeling of accomplishment subsided when he heard the soft, weak whisper of his mother from the floor beneath him.

"Baxter?" she questioned softly, still in shock from the ordeal. "What...?" she mumbled, staring at his left hand that still contained a brightly burning fire. Baxter noticed her fear and extinguished the flame with a gentle breath.

"It's ok, mom. It's over," he assured her with a calm voice. "Nothing can hurt you anymore."

"What happened?"

"You were attacked, but I'm here. I won't let anyone hurt you."

"Baxter..." her voice faded weakly as she lifted a hand from her stomach. The hand revealed a deep wound that was bleeding profusely.

"That didn't happen," Baxter spoke incredulously. "I stopped it."

"Baby..." she whispered as her voice began to falter.

"No, mom. I stopped it. You're ok. I stopped it," he repeated with tears beginning to swell in his eyes. "I saved you."

He felt a cold breeze blow through the dreamscape as his mother's eyes closed again. Her hand reached out and touched his leg before going limp and falling lifelessly to the floor.

The pain was too much, and Baxter chose to wake up.

14

THE SEND-OFF

Baxter opened his eyes to the predawn sunlight softly illuminating the small study. He felt unusual as he sat up in the cot. He hadn't so much woken up from sleep as he had simply opened his eyes from a deep, consuming reflection. Every image from the dream was still vividly imprinted on his memory. He pulled the sheets back and swung his feet to the floor.

"How'd that go?" Cassius questioned. He was reclined in Sansarev's chair and had his feet casually slung onto the desktop.

"The dream?" Baxter responded.

Cassius just continued to glare at the young man expectantly.

Baxter rubbed his arm uncomfortably. The dream didn't feel real. His control had been so complete that the experience didn't feel nearly as traumatic as his earlier nightmares, but even the thought of recalling his mother's face caused him to awkwardly hesitate. "It was scary. Intense and scary."

"Do you think Schaffer did it?" Cassius pushed.

"I don't think so. They weren't shot. I don't think Schaffer could've done it by herself."

"With help?"

"I suppose. I don't know. I just have to wait."

Cassius quickly slid his feet off the desk and motioned to the door as the sound of Sansarev coming up the stairs could be faintly heard down the adjoining corridor. Upon entering the study, the housemaster was clearly out of breath.

"Good morning, Mr. Bishop," he smiled, greeting the young man as he caught his breath. "It's been one hell of a morning."

"How's everything going?" replied the orphan. He wanted to discuss his dream with the housemaster, but he decided he'd wait to see what news the Russian had to share first.

"I just got off the phone with Detective Caine, and he confirmed that officers would be visiting St. Joseph's presently. I spoke with an old friend of mine, and he's agreed to help us with your transportation."

"My transportation?" Baxter asked curiously. "Where am I going?"

"To a place you'll be safe," responded the Russian. "He'll be picking you up this morning, so I suggest you begin gathering your belongings."

"I don't have any belongings."

The housemaster chuckled between short breaths, "Of course not. I mean we need to gather supplies. Alejandra is downstairs preparing some meals for you, and she gave me some old clothes that we can send you off with. They may not all fit that well, but they're free and in much better repair than the articles you came to us in." He chuckled again, "She decided to destroy those. I believe the various stains were too much of a bother for her to clean."

"When are they coming? Do you know?"

"We don't know. I asked Caine, but he wasn't even sure," the Russian spoke while tidying up the study. "But I was given the impression it was happening shortly. You may have noticed a touch of urgency," he laughed while expectantly glancing towards the boy who was still sitting on the cot. "For example, that cot can't be there."

Baxter quickly got the message and began cleaning up his area. "How can I help?"

"Just gather up what you can, slowly. We don't need you worsening your injuries in a rush. When you're ready, I'll meet you downstairs."

"I'll be gentle," the young man responded as he began stripping his cot. He spent the next hour or so gathering up his meager belongings along with a few outfits Sansarev had brought him. He dressed himself and paused only momentarily to appreciate the softness of the fabrics on his body. His life here was far better than he remembered the streets, but he hadn't forgotten his status with the law. There was a pulsing anxiety to his life because of it, and he wouldn't endanger the lives of anyone helping him.

When he departed the study and descended the staircase for what he imagined would be the last time, he found Sansarev waiting at the front foyer with a small sack. The Russian's expression was hidden behind his thick beard, but Baxter still detected the familiar curvature of the Russian's cheeks as his lips curled in a stubborn grin.

"You still look terrible," Sansarev commented as he held out the small sack. "Alejandra made you this. There's some good food in there. Both in terms of taste and nutrition."

"No doubt," Baxter responded cooly.

"I've also put some money in there. A good amount. Just enough to prevent trouble and not enough to cause it."

The young man smiled, "Thank you. Will I see you again?"

"I certainly hope so," chuckled Sansarev. "I'll be in touch as much as I can, safely."

15

THE FAREWELL ORPHAN

The young man could sense the urgency in the old Russian's gait, and as they continued down the drive, Baxter's eyes darted around him at the vibrant garden. Everything around him seemed like such an idyllic environment. He remembered running through the same gardens with Seth, Max, and Eliza. He remembered hiding behind the bushes and spying on Eliza long before she'd known how he felt. All the pleasant childhood memories came rushing back as he continued down the winding drive with Sansarev. The Russian's countenance was stoic, and his gaze remained transfixed on the road leading away from St. Joseph's. Once the pair had reached the end of the orphanage's grounds, Baxter saw a dark car driving up to the beginning of St. Joseph's property. Sansarev reached out and placed a firm hand on the young man's shoulder and weakly smiled. "I've arranged for a driver to take you into the city, and the payment has already been taken care of. Remember Baxter, life is about heading in the right direction. Not necessarily the easiest direction, but the direction that will eventually lead you to the right destination. You have things to offer others. You are intelligent. You are compassionate. I saw how Seth and Max looked up to you. You may not have noticed it because of your young age, but it was there. You have the ability to change people's lives for the better, and if you never use that ability, it's worse than not having it. There's nothing in the world more despicable than one who can help others and chooses not to. Nothing."

The old black car pulled up to the pair, and an old gentleman stepped out. "Sergei!" he smiled as he embraced the housemaster. His accent was foreign but different from Sansarev's thick Russian cadence. "And this must be the contraband..."

Sansarev pat Baxter on the back reassuringly, "That's right, Karel. This is my young friend, Mr. Baxter Bishop. He's fallen on tough times and needs to lay low for the time being."

"For you? Anything!" laughed the old man as he turned toward Baxter. "It's a pleasure to meet you, young man!" Karel chuckled as he shook Baxter's hand. "I'll secure your luggage in the back."

"Thank you, sir," Baxter returned, handing two medium sized duffels to his new chauffeur. He turned and firmly embraced Sansarev. "Thank you. For everything. For always letting me choose my path." He was resolute not to cry. He wanted to show Sansarev that he was becoming a man, that he was capable of shaping his destiny.

The two parted, and Baxter slid into the back seat of the automobile. Karel stepped over to Sansarev and spoke with hushed tones in a language Baxter was unfamiliar with. He'd heard Sansarev speak Russian, but this language seemed different to his ears. He assumed they must be old friends, and the housemaster was speaking in Karel's native tongue, whatever that was. He was uncertain what the men were discussing, but he had no qualms with the mysterious dialogue. He'd been drowning before, and he knew Sansarev's intentions were nothing but benevolent.

"Do svidaniya," Sansarev said as he shook Karel's hand one last time, turned, and began walking back down the winding drive to St. Joseph's. Karel stepped into the car that he'd left running, u-turned, and headed away from the orphanage. Baxter looked back through the rear window as the gardens and Sansarev's silhouette were obscured from sight.

Leaving St. Joseph's wasn't as difficult as Baxter had anticipated. In some ways, he felt a sense of adventure, although he was returning to a familiar and inhospitable situation. He hadn't developed much of a plan for where he'd go or what he'd do, but he knew he wanted to avoid the section of downtown Morristown in which he'd been assaulted. The beating he'd taken had left its wounds on his body and mind. The terror he remembered from being cornered by the gang of ruffians was something he desperately wished to avoid. His rib cage still ached, and the old suspension of Karel's vehicle caused his body to bounce uncomfortable on the worn seats.

"Karel ... that's an interesting name. I noticed you speaking a different language to Sansarev. Are you Russian?" Baxter asked, trying to make conversation.

"Oh no!" Karel laughed. "Definitely not Russian. I came here from Czechoslovakia. Karel is a common name there. It's the Czech name for this country's Charles, or Carl."

"Oh ok. How do you know Sansarev?"

"Sergei and I met a long time ago when we were both new to this country. Back in those days towns were usually divided up into neighborhoods of immigrants that came here from different regions. We first settled in a small town in America. For the smaller towns, some of the communities had numerous cultures in them. Our neighborhood was full of both Russians and people from Eastern Europe. Lots of Slavs."

"Slavs?" Baxter asked.

Karel chuckled in the mirror, "I shouldn't laugh. We always joke about Americans ignorance of geography, but really, why should you care? I love where I'm from, but it doesn't have a lot to offer. Slavs are a people from Central and Eastern Europe. They speak Slavic languages."

"I see. Sorry, I didn't know."

Karel laughed again, "No need for apologies! Where are you from?"

"Here," Baxter returned quickly hoping for no more follow up questions. His past wasn't something he could share with the same spritely attitude as Karel.

"Oh dear, I'm sorry."

"Sorry?"

"I've always felt bad for people born in America. You have such an easy life, but nothing to compare it to. How do you realize luck when you've never had misfortune?"

Baxter stood in silence staring into the rearview mirror with a look of shock on his face. The startled expression slowly gave way to a half grin.

"Hmmm," muttered Karel, "I take that back. How presumptuous of me. If you're from St. Joseph's, you must have lost your family or never knew them. That could most certainly be difficult. I can tell from your face that I misspoke."

"It's fine," Baxter grinned. He appreciated the straightforwardness of Karel. He'd become so accustomed to subtle manipulation at the hands of Schaffer and Brent that he enjoyed the alien nature of Karel's transparency.

"How did you come to stay at St. Joseph's with Sergei? If you don't mind me asking."

Baxter hesitated but decided it might benefit him to air his troubled background. "My parents died, and I was sent to St. Joseph's. I had therapy at a hospital for a while after that. Then I lived in downtown Morristown for a few months. I got mugged and went to St. Joseph's to recover but..." He trailed off. He felt a sense of normalcy that he was able to recount the tragic memories of his life in a form vague enough to at least *seem* commonplace.

"Sounds like a rocky path," Karel commented as he squinted his eyes to read a street sign.

Baxter wanted to be in an urban setting, but he also wanted to make sure he was far enough from his old location that he wouldn't risk confronting any of the gang members from his previous altercation.

Karel absently mumbled as he took a right and continued on. "I'd warn you about some of the crime down here, but from the sounds of things, you've already seen it."

"Yeah, unfortunately."

"Keep your head down. I've hoped the police would do something about the crime down here, but they seem just as disorganized as the homeless." Karel reached over to the radio and turned the volume up just a touch. Some jazz came through the car speakers, and the old man began happily tapping his fingers on the steering wheel to the tempo of the sizzling high-hat. "Do you like jazz?"

"I've never really listened to it," Baxter responded honestly.

"Nothing beats it," Karel replied so rapidly Baxter suspected he hadn't heard or cared about the young man's response. "When I listen to jazz, it feels like my heart and soul are dancing under an old streetlamp. Like they were old lovers meeting again after an eternity apart."

"I'll have to check it out sometime," the young man said as he watched his driver frantically try to keep up with the drum part.

The rest of the car ride passed with little event. Karel continued to drum on various parts of the car as the jazz continued to pour through the speakers. Baxter spent his time gazing out the window at the buildings as they passed. He'd look at the strangers on the city streets, wondering if he'd come across any familiar faces. He didn't, and he found comfort in that. He wanted this to be the beginning, a new start. Today was the day a pitiful, troubled young man died, and a brave, intelligent adult was born. He'd get a job waiting tables or working in a kitchen, and he'd make his way. He'd find a girl; he'd forget about Eliza, and he'd create a life Sansarev would be proud of. As the drive continued, he noticed the buildings were becoming increasingly worn down. The large, well-maintained apartment buildings gave way to poorly-lit, grungy tenement-style homes. The family restaurants turned into chain joints, and the sidewalks transformed from immaculate walkways to badly cracked cement paths with weeds growing in the crevices.

Eventually, Karel came up to a towering apartment building and pulled the car into a nearby side street. "How does it look?" he asked looking into the mirror.

"It? It looks great," replied a bewildered Baxter as he opened the door and began sliding out of the backseat.

"I'll grab your bags."

"Don't worry about it."

"I insist," Karel returned as he pulled the duffels out of the back. "That building look okay?" he asked pointing at the looming, dark building.

"Okay for what?"

"Okay for you to live in," Karel returned nonchalantly.

"I don't understand." Baxter's expression turned to complete confusion.

"Sergei requested that I take care of your living conditions for the first month. There is not a lot of money so this building will have to do. I'm sure you understand."

"You're going to buy me a home?" Baxter asked incredulously.

"I'm going to *rent* you a room for a month with money Sergei has provided. It is up to you to build your life from there."

Baxter turned around and once again studied the apartment building with new eyes. A surge of excitement coursed through him as he contemplated what his future may hold. Would he get a job? Would he make new friends? What adventures waited for him in the towering building?

"I know it's probably not the white picket fence home you've dreamt about, but this'll have to do for now," Karel spoke while pulling Baxter's bags out from the car's trunk. "You can wait out here. Most of the building is vacant so I'm sure I'll have an apartment number for you shortly. These places are used to having last minute tenants."

"It's fantastic," muttered Baxter in awe.

Karel chuckled, "Oh yeah, *fantastic*. I wouldn't advise staying out too late on your own in this part of town either. Once businesses started closing in the area, a lot of bad characters began hanging out around here. But I guess you should be excited. A place of your own."

"A place of my own," Baxter echoed with childish amazement.

"I'll be back in a moment, I imagine." With that, Karel headed inside the lobby of the tower.

Baxter continued to gush at what he now perceived to be a soaring spectacle of human architecture. The strong stone lines that rose up into the sky. The dark form of the building creating a profound contrast to the light blue sky above. He wondered what floor his apartment would be on; he wondered if he'd have his own bathroom, his own kitchen. He wondered if he'd have neighbors, and if he'd like them. He thought about how this would open up a new chapter in his life, a chapter free from captivity, whether legal or emotional. He paced around outside the lobby for a few minutes but eventually grew curious and started venturing further away from the main entrance. He explored the surrounding block but always kept the lobby entrance in sight. Every time anyone would exit the building, his heart would skip a beat, hoping it was Karel. He made note of the various businesses around the building. There was an old 50's style Americana diner called Sally's. Although he didn't go inside, he recognized the stereotypical neon jukebox propped up against the wall of the dining room. There was a grungy looking bar that wasn't clearly closed or open for business. Beside the bar was a bail bond office. Baxter had no idea what a bail bond was, but he assumed any office would attract honest, law-abiding citizens.

Several more minutes passed without any sight of Karel, and Baxter felt a knot of anxiety begin to swell in his stomach. He went back to the car and softly kicked the vehicle's tires while he waited. He worried the owner of the building wouldn't let him live there without an adult. He was over eighteen, but he was ignorant of any laws that might apply to this situation. He also knew he wasn't in good standing with the law. If he was checked up on by anyone, he didn't know what they'd find in the system. All the possible issues circled inside his mind like hungry vultures waiting to dine on the carcass of his hopes. The anger started to overwhelm him, and the soft taps to the tires slowly evolved into harder kicks.

"Take it easy, kid."

Baxter spun around to find Karel approaching from the lobby doorway.

"Sergei didn't give me any money to replace my hubcaps."

"Sorry," Baxter apologized. "How'd it go? You were gone for a while."

Karel rubbed the back of his neck, "The manager wasn't entirely keen on having an individual in your situation renting a place."

"Why not?"

"It's not your money. There's no guarantee for them you'll even be here next month. Under normal circumstances they'd probably decline."

"But?"

"People from poor countries know how to get what they need in shitty economies. In the end, money is king. Your security deposit and first month's rent is paid. The deposit ensures them that even if you can't pay in a month, they have some cash to take away from the deal." Karel licked his right thumb and continued to buff away a small blemish on the hood of his car. "Any questions?"

"Not that I can think of," returned Baxter. "I just go in?"

Karel laughed and handed the young man a small brass key, "Your apartment is 3C. Manager said the elevator is very old and very slow. He suggests using the stairs unless you're carrying groceries. You're a young man. It'll be good for you."

"Fine with me," Baxter laughed as he enthusiastically hefted his duffel bags onto his shoulders, only wincing slightly from his sore ribs. "Thank you, Karel. If you see Sansarev before I do, will you thank him as well?"

"Of course, though you know Sergei. He's not one for appreciation."

Baxter smiled and shook Karel's hand. He felt hopeful, like opening the lobby door was turning a page.

16

THE TOOLBOX

The building was called Stonegate, and it sat on the intersection of Fourth and Marsh. Although Baxter had wished to completely remove himself from the downtown scene, something about the city life energized him. From the countryside gardens of St. Joseph's to the isolated floodplain and sterile walls of Hothrest, the young man had spent the majority of his remembered life away from the bustle of city streets.

The actual apartment was spartan in its amenities. There was a singular window that looked out at the neighboring, apartment building's wall approximately eight feet away. Inside, there were old hardwood floors in desperate need of resurfacing and walls clad with the most hideous wallpaper available at the time of installation. To Baxter, none of these minor aesthetic blemishes mitigated his appreciation for the space. It was, after all, the first space he could consider his own, and the penny in the hand of a beggar is considerably more valuable than the coin to a prince.

Baxter enjoyed the next couple of months or so as much as he'd enjoyed any since his parents were taken from him. Sansarev had only visited once since Baxter left St. Joseph's and hadn't brought any news about his parents' case which made the nights difficult. Lying awake, staring at the ceiling, he'd picture his mother's face. The face was hazy now; uncertainty and time caused a blur to wash over what he tried to recall. Her eyes remained, but they were less vivid and less soulful than he remembered. More often than not, her visage was accompanied with fear, not their usual tenderness.

He acquired a job as a barback at the dilapidated drinking hole down the street. The establishment's sign read "The Toolbox," but only because the original proprietor had chosen to save a few bucks while renovating the old neighborhood hardware store and forewent a new sign. The bartender's name was Jade. Baxter was unsure if that was her real name; he'd never worked up the nerves to ask, and Jade's disposition didn't encourage such familiar questions. She didn't own the bar but had been dutifully slinging mind-numbing toxins since it opened. She was considered by both the clientele and employees to be the de facto owner. Her orders carried absolute authority, and her demeanor suggested obedience was in everyone's best interest.

Baxter had been a quick study. He worked hard, and his appetite for knowledge was voracious. Whether he was lending a hand fixing beer taps or clearing keg hoses, his initiative impressed Jade from day one. She took the young man under her wing and showed him everything she could about the bar business. Baxter appreciated that she never asked questions about his past. Jade told him it simply wasn't her style. She was a business woman first-and-foremost; she had no interest in her employees' personal lives, and their personal lives had no place at her bar.

Once a week, she'd allow the employees to stay at the establishment after hours for drinks, but she never stuck around for the teambuilding late night activities she allowed. Even though Baxter was still a few years away from the legal drinking age, due to these coworker get-togethers, Baxter found himself stumbling home to his apartment building completely inebriated once a week. He wasn't particularly close to any of the people he worked with. Even though he enjoyed working for Jade immensely, their relationship was built on employment, and the young man respected his boss' boundaries.

Baxter's demons stayed mostly quiet during his intoxicated periods. He found himself to generally be a happy, carefree drunk. He'd get back to his apartment, devour some inexpensive microwave dinners, and gaze out the window into the numerous apartments of the neighboring building. Over the last few months, he'd become familiar with the daily schedule of some of the people that lived in the apartments at which he'd gaze.

There was a large black family directly across from him. The man worked two jobs and was rarely home. His wife worked a night shift that began around the time Baxter would get back from The Toolbox, and she'd stay home with their three daughters and two sons during the day. The apartment seemed entirely too small for such a large family, but Baxter rarely saw any serious disagreements between the family members. Occasionally one of the boys or girls would tease a sibling, and the apartment would transform into a disturbed ant nest with children shooting from room to room chasing whoever the instigator was for that particular argument.

In one of the apartments a story above his own was a single young lady who Baxter presumed was in her late twenties or early thirties. Baxter found her to be very attractive, and he'd occasionally peek up at her window in hopes of catching her preparing for bed or otherwise indisposed. He wasn't proud of his surveillance, but he attributed it to adolescent nature and refused to judge himself too severely for violating her privacy. He'd even seen her a couple of times walking around the neighborhood but had never worked up the courage to say hello. How embarrassing he thought it would be if she recognized him as the gawking little pervert from across the alley.

Those were the only windows that Baxter found truly interesting to survey during his late nights alone in his apartment. He hadn't made any friends in his building as most of the other tenants kept to themselves; the only greetings exchanged would be surly grunts from the men and awkward, darting glances from the women. The only social occasions for the young man came after intense evenings of drinking at The Toolbox when Cassius would visit his apartment. The visits were generally a welcomed distraction from the otherwise perpetual solitude. Cassius' drop-ins had become more common, and Baxter assumed their frequency was a byproduct of his loneliness. Cassius would occasionally drop by the bar, but he never interrupted Baxter's work. He'd simply stay in the shadows or help himself to a game of pool at the old table along the back wall.

One night, well after two as the bar was shutting down, Baxter made the mistake of participating in a conversation with Cassius about the pool table's desperate need of a re-felted surface; however, after a stern, suspicious look from Jade, he quickly picked up his bar rag and hurried back to bussing empty shot and pint glasses from the nearby bar corner.

"You alright, kid?" questioned Jade.

"Fine," laughed Baxter nervously. "Nothing more embarrassing than being caught mumbling to yourself."

She accepted the explanation and turned back to shooing off a couple of tipsy regulars who were obnoxiously whining about the injustice of last call. The young man finished wiping down the tables and ran back to Jade's side to see if there were any other side jobs with which he could assist.

She smiled and chuckled, "Nothing else I can't handle, Bax. Thanks for the help this evening. Last thing I have to do is get these two drunk bastards out of here so I can get home." She made sure both her customers overheard the conversation before she shot a half-playful, half-menacing glare in their direction. The two locals took the hint, clinked their glasses, and downed the remaining swigs of their pints.

"See that?" Jade mused, "We're all done for the evening."

Baxter let out a soft snicker as the bar door closed behind the two men, "Guess I'll be heading home then."

"Hold up a tick," the bartendress called as he began his departure. "It's been a long day. Have a drink with me?"

Baxter paused briefly as drinking with Jade was an unusual occurrence for the staff. She didn't mind them having a few beers after hours, but it rarely included her company. "Sure," he answered. "That'd be nice."

Jade laughed at his response as she grabbed two pint glasses and two shot glasses. "If you're not careful, you'll end up speaking to yourself a lot more in this line of work than you should. You start spending too much time around people with nothing to say, and you begin having to entertain yourself to stave off the idiocy of it all."

"I've always talked to myself," Baxter responded with a trace of defensiveness. "At least since as long as I can remember."

"Then you're prone to it and will have to work extra hard not to become a total hermit!" Jade teased with a wide grin. She slid the beer and a shot of Jameson across the bar to Baxter while holding up her own shot glass in salute. "To drunken idiots, and the livelihood they supply for us!"

Baxter clinked glasses and laughed, "Cheers!" Jade polished her shot off with the ease of a long time server, while Baxter struggled greatly as the potent liquor rebelled against his taste buds. He coughed a few times and rubbed his throat.

"It takes practice," joked Jade as she filled up both glasses again. "Perseverance, training, and finally, *integrity!*" She burst into laughter at her sarcasm before swiftly tossing the second shot back. She glanced intently at Baxter's remaining liquor.

"Give me a second," the young man responded to her stare. His mouth had begun salivating, and he feared another shot without a break could end up being more embarrassing than falling behind.

"Don't kill yourself, Bax. I've been at this for a *long* time. No need to stress over it."

"No, no, I'm fine," the young man mustered up the bravery and fought down the saliva to attempt the other shot. It went down smoother than the first but still caused Baxter to cough and widen his eyes to keep them from tearing up.

"I've noticed you've been spending a lot of time working. I don't normally get into it with my staff, but don't you have other places you'd like to be?" Jade filled up her shot glass, and after a brief hesitation, filled up Baxter's as well.

"I like it here," the young man responded. "It keeps my mind off other stuff. Keeps me focused on more important things."

"Cleaning up beer rings on tables and stocking my bar are important things?" Jade snickered, "What an employee!"

"I mean staying out of trouble is an important thing."

"I figured there was stuff in your past you were running from," she said with greater tenderness. "I s'pose we all do. Good on ya."

"Yeah ..." Baxter trailed off dismissively.

"I'm serious! People always talk shit about running from your problems, but in my experience, that's damn near the best thing you can do." A well-hidden Southern accent was slowly being added to Jade's speech with every shot of Jameson she tossed down. "It's important to separate the problems you can solve from the one's you can't. Don't spend your time tryin' to fix the unfixable. Best just run from 'em. But really, how can a kid like you really have it that bad? Run away from home?"

Baxter felt apprehensive. He thought Jade may be an uncommon soul who could sympathize with his situation, but he didn't want to risk it. Regardless of her capacity for sympathy, he could never tell her the whole truth; his story was bound to make anyone suspicious.

"Didn't runaway. Haven't had a home for a long time," he responded with a surly tone. He didn't like being called a kid, but he assumed it was just Jade's way of speaking. He'd heard her refer to much older customers as kids as well. "I'm an orphan." He stopped there, hoping that would be the end of any further questions.

"Frequently?" Jade smiled as she held back laughter.

"What?"

"Nevermind," she chuckled to herself. "It's a joke from my favorite musical."

"Uh, right."

"I bet that's a tough gig. Being an orphan. I had parents, but they weren't the kind you'd want. Father was a drunk. I should say *mean* drunk. Nothing wrong with drinking alone. It's what you can become; that's the rub." After buffing a troublesome spot out of the bar with a rag, she filled up another shot glass and continued, "Used to beat me and my brother up pretty bad after he got home from the local AA meeting." She looked out one of the bar windows into the night for a moment as if remembering a specific memory with a revitalized nostalgia. "He would've been a great example of irony if his bullshit story wasn't so cliche."

In his own effort to display empathy, Baxter downed another shot of Jameson, trying not to sneer at the taste.

"Just sayin', sometimes having parents isn't always a walk through a candy store."

"No, I guess not," Baxter replied hoping to end the conversation there. "I should be getting home soon. I open tomorrow morning."

"You're kidding? You *do* work like a dog. One more for the road?" she asked and filled up her glass a final time.

"Sure," Baxter answered with poorly masked regret as

he watched the dark amber liquid quickly fill up his glass. "One more," he whispered.

"You don't have to!"

"One more," he repeated.

The glasses clinked, the whiskey was consumed, and the two empty vessels hit the bar with a single dull thud. Baxter dismounted from his bar stool and took a few uneasy steps toward the door before calibrating his equilibrium and making his way out. Jade simply put the Jameson away and gazed out after her bar-back.

17

RETOX

The streets were empty when Baxter drunkenly stumbled out of The Toolbox. A cool breeze pushed an empty plastic bag down the center of the street, and the young man watched it as it disappeared from view down a dimly lit alley. He took in a deep breath before beginning his disorganized march down the sidewalk toward Stonegate. He hadn't walked more than a couple of stores down from the bar when he heard a sharp whisper coming from another nearby side street.

"Baxter? That you? I knew I'd seen you go into that bar..." The side street had no lights, making it impossible to determine the identity of the voice's owner. Baxter squinted his eyes in order to focus further into the darkness but still couldn't make out a face. Eventually the form grew larger as it departed the shadows of the alley and entered the dim street lights of the main road.

"Stretch!?" Baxter called out in shock as his old

acquaintance came out of the alley. "What are you doing here?"

"I do some business over here every now and then. I thought I'd seen you earlier today when you went into that bar, but I wasn't sure. I stuck around and waited for the people to leave, but you still didn't come out. I went over to the front and heard your voice from the inside. Didn't know who you were talking to after the bar had closed, but I figured I'd wait here in the alley to see how you were." Stretch's face took on a tone of sincere embarrassment. "I heard about those guys that came by my place when you were there. I heard about what happened. Sorry, man."

Baxter's teeth grit with a combination of pain and his own humiliation. "Don't worry about it. It happened. Didn't have anything to do with you ... did it?"

"Hell no! You know I'd never get messed up with those assholes."

"Yeah, I know. I'm lucky I walked away from that," Baxter offered optimistically.

"For real."

"What have you been doing? Are you selling drugs?"

"Gotta make some cash. Stay afloat, ya know?" Stretch pushed his right hand across his nose and rubbed it vigorously. "Have you done any since our trip downtown?"

"No. My experience with that mess wasn't one I care to repeat."

Stretch laughed, "Hey man, you can't blame yourself for those assholes. Wrong place, wrong time. That's all."

"I don't want to be in the wrong place again."

"You live 'round here?" Stretch asked with uncertainty. He didn't know why, but he felt unsure Baxter would feel comfortable even divulging the address of his new home.

"Yeah. Stonegate," answered Baxter, pointing up the street to his building.

"Damn, son! Nice! How'd you swing that? Where'd you get the cash?"

"An old friend."

"Good to have friends, am I right?"

"Yeah," Baxter responded flatly.

"Speaking of friends, I finished all my deliveries down here, and I've got a little extra if you're interested?"

Baxter laughed, "No, that's alright. But thanks." Deep down the warm feelings from the Jameson pushed him to accept, but the horrible memory of the gang assault kept him from indulging.

"You sure?" his friend pushed.

"Yeah."

"Alright, alright. Won't force you. But hey man I hope I see you 'round. No hard feelings about those bastards, right?"

"None," Baxter agreed with a drunk smile.

"Alright good. Well I'll catch you another time." Stretch turned down the road and began departing before wheeling around quickly, "Hey Baxter!"

"Yeah?"

"If you ever feel like takin' another trip." Stretch tossed a small bag through the air to Baxter. "It's on me, right?"

Before the orphan had a chance to decline, the dealer

had turned away and was swiftly making his way down the main strip, passing The Toolbox with an excited whistle. Baxter looked down at the clear bag full of small yellow chunks and thought to immediately toss the stuff away, but instead, he pushed the bag into his vest pocket and continued on to Stonegate.

When Baxter reached his apartment, he removed the bag of crystalline chunks and tossed his vest on the floor beside his mattress. He still felt the warm embrace of the whiskey filling his mind with a smooth confidence. He wanted to take a hit, but he also remembered his agreement with Sansarev. He hadn't *truly* agreed to anything, but he knew the housemaster who'd given him so much would be severely disappointed with him getting involved with drugs or Stretch in general. He sat on his mattress and opened the small clear bag. He thought about his time in downtown Morristown. He thought about the gang that had attacked him. They'd almost killed him. His ribs had fully healed, but the memory of the beating caused a phantom pain to dance down his rib cage. *These drugs have caused you a fair amount of pain in the past.* The thoughts echoed in his head, but he rationalized the emotions. *The drugs weren't the cause of that assault. If you'd never touched the stuff Stretch gave you, they still would've been there, and they still would kicked the shit out of you.*

Baxter placed the open bag on the floor beside his

bed. He figured it would be easier to refrain from using if the bag wasn't in his hands. He kicked his shoes off and fell back onto his mattress, staring up at the ceiling and rubbing his eyes.

"Funny seeing Stretch out there," Cassius muttered from the corner of the room.

"Yeah. I know I shouldn't blame him for what happened but remembering that day causes so much pain and hate." The young man touched the side of his torso where the ribs had cracked.

"It *did* take you back to St. Joseph's. That was a good thing, right?"

"I guess. I would've seen Sansarev again anyways. Probably in better condition." Baxter leaned up from his bed and looked over to his older friend. "Have you ever done any drugs, Cassius?"

The older man chuckled, "Yeah, I've messed around with some stuff, but I don't encourage it. It's dangerous messing with your mind like that. I s'pose you kind of get used to feeling fuzzy at Hothrest. Never in your right mind."

Baxter's stare once again fixated on the small clear bag. He still felt in high spirits from the whiskey, but he knew he wouldn't be able to fall asleep. He picked up the small clear bag and noticed Stretch had left a miniature glass pipe in the bag with the yellow rocks. Baxter remembered the feeling, the euphoria. He glanced over at Cassius for an affirmative gesture, but his friend's facial expression remained completely indifferent. "It feels kinda nice to be in a safe place now." He carefully pulled the glass instrument out of the bag and examined it with a mixture of curiosity, fear, and intrigue.

"No gangs in your apartment. That's for sure," Cassius chuckled in an upbeat manner as he gazed out the window. All the neighboring apartments were dark as their tenants slept safely in their homes. He turned to the young man on the bed, and his face became slightly more stern, "But don't start thinkin' that just because you're alone, you're safe. Bad things can happen to a man when he's alone with his thoughts if they get dark enough."

"I'm good, Cassius," Baxter stated dismissively. "I've never been in a better place than I am now. It's not like using this stuff to calm my mind is a new thing for me. No one was judging me for using drugs at Hothrest."

"Is it the same?"

"No, it's not, and I know that," Baxter responded as if immediately caving on his own argument before replying, "But it's not as different as everyone's saying, is it? I mean, a drug is a drug, right? Some have different effects on your mind, but that's what they all do. They make you feel different: tired, happy, excited, relaxed, all different feelings, but they're all just that. Making your brain feel different."

Cassius remained silent.

"And don't judge me, Cassius," the young man's tone became defensive. "You were at Hothrest. You've been in my boat for a *long* time. I bet you've taken all sorts of pills they gave you, and I bet you had *no* idea what any of them were. I've done *this* before, and I know how it makes me feel. It makes me feel much better than anything Brent ever gave me."

Cassius' eyes left the young man and returned to their observation of the neighboring building. For a moment, he was as cold and unresponsive as the dark windows, holding their thoughts and stories within, but eventually he spoke. "I don't think what you're doing is *wrong*, Baxter. I think it's dangerous. We've done lots of dangerous stuff, and I'm happy you're in your own home now. A safe place. That doesn't make it safe though. It's a tough world. You've come to learn that in a more difficult way than most, but don't let life fool you. Sometimes the things that make us feel the best are the worst for us."

"You're probably right," Baxter confessed, "But sometimes they're just breaks. Vacations from reality." He placed a rock in the pipe. "I've worked hard to get here." His eyes narrowed slightly as he struck the match and put his lips to the pipe. The yellow rocks began to melt, and Baxter closed his eyes. "I deserve a vacation," he breathed calmly.

As the smoke filled the young man's lungs, he felt the familiar euphoria overtake him. His body felt lighter, and a renewed energy began to pulse through his muscles. He smiled and leaned back on the soft cloud-like cushion his thin mattress had become. A pleasurable warmth spread from his heart all the way out to the tips of each extremity, and his fingers began tingling as they quickly slid back and forth on the sheets. He exhaled slowly, feeling the breath work its way from his lungs out of his mouth in an invigorating parade of wind. He glanced over to the window where Cassius had been stationed, but his old friend had gone, slipped into the night as mysteriously as he ever appeared. Baxter swiftly bounced up from his mattress and traversed the room to check out the neighboring apartments from his window. His eyes were beginning to dart to every edge of his vision as he searched the environment for something to hold his rapidly shifting attention, but all the lights in the adjacent building were off. He desperately wished the girl across the alley had been awake as the alcohol had granted him the confidence to attempt communication, but there were no signs of life from her dark window. After an hour or so, Baxter began to feel his high subside, and he too, decided it was time for rest. He opened the bar tomorrow, and he'd hate to let Jade down the morning after she'd been so kind. Before he turned away from the window, he noticed a darker shadow shoot past the building a few stories below. The dark, blurry apparition caused a shiver to run down his arms, and he quickly averted his gaze. He didn't want the subsiding high to push his restful sleep into a fearful state.

He returned to his mattress and slid himself under the sheets. Although they were cheap, they provided a sense of security he desperately desired as his mind calibrated itself to the departing drugs. He reached over and flicked the switch on his bedside lamp and exhaled sharply as the room went dark. The only trace of light came from the new moon's soft, silver glow on the window sill. As his eyes closed, the silver lining vanished, and he quickly slipped into slumber, exhausted by the events of the night.

18

COUNCIL OF THE HOPELESS

B axter felt a cold chill run up his spine as he pressed his back against the wrought iron post behind him. The ground was soaked and sheets of rain continued to fall from the eerily dark and densely overcast sky above. Every few seconds, a strong gust would whip his clothing tightly against his body, and as the soaked clothes pressed against his skin, he'd clutch his arms together and shiver against the metal post. He scanned his surroundings, trying to take in every aspect of the dreamscape he could, but his vision eventually rested on the iron gate that he'd been sitting against. Hanging from two heavy metal chains was a massive sign that read, "*Cemetary*" in large Old English letters. The imposing sign hung precariously on worn, rusted hinges and appeared that it may break free of its supports and crash into the muddy puddles beneath.

The young man decided to cautiously slip past the metal post he'd leaned on and make his way into the graveyard. His subconscious spurred him forward to explore some of the more impressive tombstones scattered throughout the grounds. Some graves were marked with modest stones and brief passages concerning the lives of those residing beneath; others were marked with massive structures celebrating the corpses of better men. Many of these mausoleums were lavishly decorated with ornate gargoyles or gothic steeples that stretched into the overcast sky. Baxter acknowledged the atmosphere was certainly a bad omen for a dream, but a desperate curiosity pushed the young man deeper into the rows of stone markers.

"Cawww!" called a crow as it shot overhead in a hurry to escape the downpour. Baxter was reminded of his previous dream where a similar bird soared through a massive library. The previous blackbird seemed much more majestic than the current beast which seemed only desperate to find shelter from the deluge.

Baxter's eyes scanned the tombstones for anything that would help him decipher why he was here or what his subconscious might be trying to tell him. His vision finally rested on one large stone surrounded by rougher brush off to the side of the tidy cemetery rows. He gently pulled the wet clothing from his body and slowly approached the grave as sheets of rain continued to fall. The grave appeared to have been recently dug as the dirt that covered its contents was free of flora. Baxter knelt in the puddle of muddy water and wiped rain from his brow in order to discern the epitaph. Discovering his parents' names on the stone didn't surprise him in the least. He would have been far more confused had the grave contained the names of strangers; however, his next actions shocked the dreamer as they felt completely involuntary. His hands fell down on the muddy soil and began digging in a voracious manner. His fingers repeatedly sank into the mud and threw large handfuls of earth away from the gravesite. Sweat ran down the dreamer's face as he dug deeper into the ground in a frenzied, uncontrollable manner. The mission to clear the hole of dirt seemed futile, as the rain continued to flood the pit with muddy water. Eventually, his nails clawed against the wood of a coffin within the grave. He continued to clear mud until he was able to pry the top from the thick, pine box, but the young man stood puzzled as water and mud poured into what he discovered was an empty coffin. Thunder boomed from overhead, and seconds later, a lightning bolt illuminated the box briefly, but only to confirm that it was indeed empty. The young man pressed his palms against the floor of the coffin, searching for anything that could provide meaning to the dream, but his palms slid across the soaked, sanded bottom of the box. He sat in the grave, confounded and frustrated, until another boom of thunder struck overhead, and its accompanying flash of lightning, once again, lit up the scene. Everything around him was bathed in light except for a shadow that exclusively covered the dreamer in darkness. From the grave, Baxter looked overhead to identify what had cast the lonely shadow, and he beheld a towering being covered in a heavy black cloak. Although the heavy rain falling onto his face made it difficult to discern much else from the figure, he did recognize his own eyes staring out from the shadows of the cloak's cowl.

"Where are they?!" the dreamer shouted at the shadowy figure as another lightning bolt bathed the cloak's silhouette in a lurid glow.

"They are gone, and their memories are of no consequence. Only you remain: looking but unable to see, searching but unable to find," the cloaked figure hissed as it knelt closer to the grave. "We find you hopeless. We watch as you rattle the bars of your cage and drown in the flood. We watch as you remain frozen in a moving world; a broken soul that can only fixate on the origins of its disrepair. You sacrifice without benefit; you wander without destination, and you *are* lost. Blind to time and deaf to hope. I will leave you now. There is nothing in this cemetery but emptiness, and nothing in this grave digger but self-pity."

"I command you!" Baxter shouted at the phantom with the fleeting courage he could muster, but as the words left his mouth, even he could hear the undertones of fear.

The phantom emitted a sinisterly mocking laugh at the young man, "You are not worthy of command. I bring truth, and I do not heed pawns. Awaken hopeless one!"

19

FATHERHOOD

Baxter woke up angry. He was unsure if his mood was caused by the hangover, his inability to control his dream, the ridicule of the phantom, or if it was simply born from the realization that he was scheduled to open The Toolbox at noon. By both fantasy and reality, he had developed a cantankerous mood, and the mocking words of the apparition from his dream profoundly aggravated him. He had demonstrated such impressive control and power during his previous reverie concerning his parents; it was discouraging that he'd been so helpless when ridiculed by the apparition's cryptic message.

He lay face up on his meager mattress for several minutes glaring peevishly at the ceiling before he heard a tapping at his chamber door. He grumpily rose from the bed, made his way across the cramped apartment, and cracked open the door to investigate who would be visiting him this early in the morning. He rarely had recreational visitors. Occasionally, a custodian or repairman from the building would drop by to announce some inspection or repair a pipe clanging in the wall, but as the young man peeked past the chain lock, he was pleasantly surprised to see Sansarev, standing in the hallway clothed in an inconspicuous hooded sweatshirt.

"May I come in?" the Russian asked with a smirk.

"Sansarev!" Baxter exclaimed with surprised joy as he unfastened the chain from the doorframe. The Russian entered, and Baxter happily embraced his old housemaster. "What brings you to the city?" the young man asked, although he assumed he was the answer.

"You, my dear boy!" responded Sansarev in his typically ebullient tone. "Karel told me you've been maintaining employment at that drinking hole down the block, which I'm thrilled to hear. I worked at a pivnaya on the outskirts of Moscow when around your age. It taught me some very important lessons concerning the recklessness of man." The Russian made himself comfortable in the meager apartment as he jokingly grimaced at the young man's slovenly dwelling. "Think you may benefit from a housekeeper. Alejandra would be mortified to see your mess in here." As Sansarev gently chastised Baxter, he slowly continued to survey the apartment until he noticed the small pipe beside the young man's mattress. He knelt and grasped the glass piece before meticulously examining its contents. His brow furrowed is disappointment, and he turned to confront the boy. "Mr. Bishop, what is this?"

Baxter froze, petrified with fear that his transgression

had been discovered. The fear of Sansarev's justice scared the boy; however, the much greater anxiety came only moments later, when the old Russian's face transformed from palpable anger to profound disappointment. "Sansarev, I-" he began, but he was swiftly and coldly cut off by his benefactor.

"Don't…don't give me excuses, Baxter. I don't care for them." He rubbed his eyes in exasperation before continuing, "Our lives are made up of what happens to us and how we respond to those things. I've always believed in you, and I've always stood up for you when the unforeseen snares of life hooked you, but there is more to fate, more to destiny, then simply throwing our hands up in frustration at the perceived injustices of the world. We can fight. We can live our best. We can promote what is good and decent in this world. Hard work, honesty, integrity; virtues that every man and woman can stand behind. This-" he spat, gesturing toward the glass pipe, "This is inviting tragedy into your home, and I will not use my time supporting someone who is so eager to invite tragedy." During his monologue, the Russian's face switched between the confounded and disappointed expression from earlier and an unnerving aggravation that bubbled under the surface.

The disappointment hit Baxter the hardest. He genuinely admired and respected Sansarev, and he immediately felt the pangs of regret for having let his old housemaster down. The Russian's stern gaze burned into his young protégé while Baxter cast a remorseful glare down to his feet and mumbled, "I'm sorry, Sansarev. My friend, Stretch, gave it to me last night after I finished closing The Toolbox. I don't normally do things like that, but I felt like it couldn't hurt anything yesterday. I shouldn't have done it, but it didn't hurt anything," he offered apologetically.

"It didn't hurt anything *today*, you mean," corrected the Russian. "It reinforces your readiness to gamble on your future. You convinced yourself it isn't going to hurt you *this* time. But you're also fully aware that it's habit-forming. Those people all began with your same rationalization. That it didn't immediately hurt them so it must be harmless. The streets out there are littered with people who didn't have the strength to simply say no, and instead, they're left searching for something that's slowly destroying them. It hurt you; you just haven't realized the damage yet." Sansarev closely examined the pipe before dropping it to the floor and briskly dropping his heel down onto the piece. The pipe shattered under his heavy boot, and he kept the boot on top of the broken shards for a long moment as if to accentuate the conviction of his views. "If you want more, go find more."

A tear of shame rolled down Baxter's cheek. His unplanned rendezvous with his treasured mentor had turned into a severe scolding that devastated the young man. He felt childish and immature, and he hated it. He furiously wiped away the tear from his cheek and took a deep breath. Sansarev recognized the young man's dejection and placed his hand gently on his shoulder.

"I'm only hard on you because of how much I care,

Mr. Bishop," the Russian said in a sympathetic tone. "I hope you understand that."

Baxter nodded but remained silent.

"There was another reason I came to visit you rather than to tongue-lash you over this unfortunate hiccup," Sansarev continued with a more jovial tone to bring some levity to the conversation.

Baxter willingly took the bait and attempted a weak smile, "Yeah, what's up?"

"Both Fenway and Schaffer have been released under their own recognizance."

"Recognizance? What does that mean?" questioned the young man.

"It means they're allowed to leave the station but will need to return at a later date. Probably after more evidence has been discovered. Apparently, the informant that fingered Fenway had enough going on in his criminal history that he wouldn't stand up to much scrutiny. This is all according to Detective Caine; he's still asking about you." Sansarev pulled his pipe out of his jacket and gave a pleading glance to Baxter. "Do you mind?"

The question was a bit awkward considering the previous chastisement; however, the young man nodded with a guilty smirk, "Make yourself comfortable. What happens now?"

"Caine was dreadfully aggravated last time we spoke," responded Sansarev. "I don't think he's particularly fond of how the department is handling Fenway's case, but he called it. He knew it would be a difficult story to stick to someone connected to the system."

"You think they let him go because he's a lawyer?"

"I'm sure that's not the reason, but I imagine it has something to do with it. They didn't really have that much information or evidence to go on, but I'd put money on something going on there."

"Has Caine learned anything new from either of them?" the young man questioned.

"I honestly don't have much of the inside information on it," Sansarev conceded, "There are many things Caine can't talk about, and no one knows what Schaffer has discussed with her lawyer. I don't think anyone knows where this is going, but it's not going to be a quickly resolved situation."

"I wish I knew what Schaffer's story was," Baxter mused.

"What happened that night..." the Russian trailed off, "I just can't imagine Dr. Schaffer doing it. I don't mean that she seems so nice that she couldn't commit a crime; I'm aware that everyone has the capacity for great evil. This may come off as sexist, but I just don't see an untrained woman being able to, you know, physically accomplish such a task without any injuries of their own. There must have been a fight of some kind; even with a knife, I just don't see a lone woman causing that much havoc and walking away relatively unscathed. That's what I've been rolling around in my melon," the housemaster muttered as he tapped his forehead.

"I've thought about that too. I had a dream..." Baxter trailed off, uncertain if he wanted to recount the entirety of his previous dream of that night; however after brief hesitation, he decided it could be helpful for him to get it off his chest. "I had a dream about that night a ways back. The whole thing, with the broken window, and both my parents being there. It just seemed like something a man would have had to do."

"Both your parents being there..." Sansarev murmured as he stroked his beard pensively.

"What about it?" Baxter returned, feeling slightly unnerved by his mentor's tone.

"You're certain they were both there?"

"Yes."

"I mean that they were always both there?"

"Always?" the young man responded, thoroughly lost.

"You told me you were in bed when it happened, right?"

"I was sleeping. It was late."

"So you don't know if your dad was there in the beginning of the event?"

Baxter paused in thought. He'd never queried his father's presence at the conflict. His body had been there, so of course he was present. Sansarev's line of questioning pushed him to consider possibilities he'd never considered. *What if he hadn't been?*

His mother's body had been surrounded by evidence of violence: the pool of blood, the shattered window, the fear in her eyes. The recollection of his mother lying there made him feel physically ill.

His father's body was bizarrely absent of the same type of evidence. He didn't remember any pools of blood or deep stains on the blanket that seemed to almost peace-fully cover him. There were no clear indicators of a strug-gle. He'd lacked the fortitude to look into his father's face for an expression, although in retrospect, he wished he had.

"Baxter?" Sansarev spoke while snapping his finger. The young man had been lost in thought as he recalled the grizzly night.

"Sorry," he spoke dazedly, "I was just remembering. It was so horrible; I always just wanted to forget that night completely. When I think back, it doesn't all seem to make sense." Baxter recounted the bizarre discrepancies be-tween his mother and father's bodies while Sansarev lis-tened intently.

"So are you still sure that your father was there the en-tire time?" the housemaster prodded gently.

"What else could have happened?"

"Think about it. It's bizarre that your father was seem-ingly unable to fend off an attacker, and on top of that, there doesn't seem to be any clear evidence that your fa-ther *did*, in fact, put up much of a struggle. In the case of your mother, something sinister must have definitely taken place, but your father...? I've been holding onto the idea that of course Schaffer couldn't have done this. Even with a knife, she couldn't dispatch a fully grown man with-out a struggle."

Baxter cleared his throat uncomfortably, "So what do you think could have happened?"

Sansarev shook his head with frustration, "I have no

idea. My thoughts haven't led me toward what may have happened as much as how little sense it all seems to make. I'm sorry, Mr. Bishop. I know I've only added more questions without answers."

"That night has been in the back of my mind my whole life. I don't imagine it's ever going to change. I just want the truth to come out. I've reached the point where I don't even care what that truth is."

"I don't envy that position," commented his mentor. "I don't blame you, but I hope the truth you discover grants you at least some degree of salvation. I'd hate for these coming revelations to cause you more anguish. Prepare for the worst, Mr. Bishop. Hope for the best but prepare for the worst. Try to keep your head above water. I'm bringing a couple of surprises for you next week. I think they'll buoy your spirits."

20

FROM CHESTERPOL WITH LOVE

Baxter had to run to The Toolbox in order to begin opening the bar on time. As he approached the building, he glanced around the streets for any sight of Stretch. He knew his friend would be back at some point but was unsure when his elusive dealer would make an appearance. Jade kept the bar keys in a combination-locked, iron box on the side of the entrance way. She'd frequently complain about crime in the area, and upon being named manager of the establishment, had immediately upgraded the seedy venue's security systems.

He enjoyed opening the bar. The first thing he always did upon arriving at work was to start up the jukebox. He found music helped clear his mind of the cobwebs of negativity that would frequently encumber him after conversations concerning the fate of his parents. Once the soulful notes of Sam Cooke began flooding the room, he started pulling stools off the bar and chairs off the tables.

He placed a cutting board out and began slicing the lemons and limes, nodding his head to the beat and doing his best not to focus on his previous conversation with Sansarev. He wasn't more than a few minutes into cutting up the bar fruit before Cassius piped up from one of the back pool tables. "Sam Cooke! Yes, please!" he laughed.

"Hey Cassius," Baxter smiled while continuing to deftly slice the fruit.

"I think Sansarev was on to something back there," his old friend said with a thoughtful tone. "Never thought about it much, but it certainly seems crazy. I know no woman is going to put this man down without a tumble."

"I just want it all to be over. I'm making something of myself out here. I'm tired of being defined by my past."

"Boy, we're all defined by our pasts. Our futures aren't written yet. Best get used to it. I've been thinking about what that creepy old Russian was saying though. Maybe your pops decided to end it all himself. Maybe your mom found out about the whole affair and was furious with the old dog. He took her life and finished himself off, nice and easy."

"Shut up, man. You have no idea what you're talking about," Baxter snapped pointing the dull bar knife at his friend.

"Take it easy, sweetie," Cassius cooed with mocking sensitivity. "I thought you wanted to solve this stuff. Seems to me that you're too worried about finding something dark about your precious mom and pop to really solve much of anything."

"He was cheating on her. I know that. Suicide doesn't make any sense. The window was broken into. I know they were involved, just not how exactly, yet." Baxter began slicing the lemons with a faster pace, growing frustrated at Cassius' hypotheses.

"You really don't think your father had any involvement with it?" Cassius chuckled, "That is some wishful thinking if I ever heard any!" The older man racked up the balls on a pool table and began playing a game. "Think about it for a second. You stumble on that type of scene. Your mom is strewn across the floor, lying in a pool of blood. Shattered glass everywhere. Terror in her eyes. Then there's your pops. Cuddled up in the blankets, like he didn't even wake up when all that commotion was going on. No broken bed posts, no upturned nightstand on his side. If you hadn't gone down there that night, you wouldn't even have known your pops was dead. He could've slept there for a couple more days before anyone smelled anything," Cassius laughed hysterically while he paced the table looking for easy shots, "Seven ball, that corner."

"Maybe he was sleeping when they first came in. Maybe he was the first. Maybe the window broke on the way out," Baxter reasoned with his friend.

"The shattered glass was *inside*. If they'd broken the window jumping out, there would've been glass on the *outside*. Three in the side."

"Maybe they threw something through the window to make it look like that. There are a lot of possibilities for what could have happened. There's no point in obsessing over it. We don't even know what Schaffer's story is. I'm sure those lawyers have multiple explanations as to how everything went down. We'll find out when they tell us."

"You're willing to wait?"

"I don't have a choice. No other way to find out," the young man calmly replied as he replaced the bar's spill mats.

"Dirty, nine off the two, right there. Do you think your dad is innocent?"

"I think he was cheating. I don't think he killed anyone."

"Sure seems suspicious," Cassius muttered under his breath as he re-chalked his cue.

Baxter rolled his eyes and headed to the back to load up the ice bins. He heard the front door open and hurried to the front to see who'd come in. It was Stretch, and he let out a toothy grin as he recognized Baxter behind the bar.

"Hey, hey man," Stretch greeted Baxter while clapping his hands together, "I know you mentioned you had to work early this morning. Figured I'd drop in and see how you're livin'."

"We're not open yet," Baxter replied coldly. Although he knew his surrender to drugs was his own fault, it felt much easier to share some of the blame with Stretch. "I'll get in trouble if the boss comes in and sees you here."

"You really think she'll care? It's that girl with dark hair I see come in here all the time, right?"

"Yeah, Jade," Baxter returned as he wiped down the bar.

"How's she?"

"She's nice."

"I mean how is she? You know."

"She's nice, and she's a friend," Baxter returned feeling slightly more annoyed with Stretch.

"I think this guy really enjoys hearing himself talk," snickered Cassius. "Boom!" he exclaimed as he banked the four ball into a corner.

Baxter slung the bar rag over his shoulder, "Sorry Stretch, but you're gonna have to go. I can't have visitors in here before the bar opens."

"Yeah, yeah, it's cool. How was that shit I gave you yesterday? Pretty good, right?" Although Stretch had acknowledged Baxter's rules, he slowly took a few steps closer to the bar. "It was some of my best stuff."

"I shouldn't be doing that stuff," Baxter returned. He contemplated bringing up Sansarev but decided it was superfluous information.

"Hey man, if it doesn't relax you then by all means don't do it. Stress is bad for you, and it helps me relieve stress. Why you so uptight about it?"

"I'm not uptight about it. I've just taken lots of drugs in my past, and they haven't helped me."

Stretch sat on one of the stools and eagerly dropped his elbows onto the bar, "What do you mean you've taken lots of drugs in your past?"

"Don't want to talk about it, but I have. And you can't stay here, don't make yourself comfortable. Jade should be coming in anytime now, and I'm not getting in trouble because you can't take a hint."

"Alright brother, no need to get angsty at me 'bout it." He slid off the stool in a sluggish manner and sauntered toward the door, "Whenever you get a chance though, either just bring that stuff back to me or throw me fifty bucks when you can."

"Throw you fifty-?" Baxter started to call out, but Stretch had already slipped out the door.

"Boy, you gettin' hustled," laughed Cassius as he blasted the eight ball into a corner. "You better watch that kid. He's bringin' trouble with him."

Jade arrived at the bar about an hour after Stretch had departed. She whistled happily as she inspected Baxter's work from the morning. He'd been a quick apprentice at The Toolbox, and she felt an immense sense of satisfaction from his performance as she considered him her promising pupil. "How'd everything go last night? Did you have any trouble opening up this morning? I was worried you may have had a bit of a hanger on."

"Nope, nothing bad. The housemaster from my old orphanage dropped by the apartment and spent the early morning with me which was nice," he answered as he absent-mindedly wiped the bar.

Jade plopped her bag down on the bar and spoke while she braided her hair, "It's nice that you still have a relationship with him. He treats you well?"

"Better than I deserve."

Jade laughed, "Don't say that, Baxter! You deserve an easier life than you've got. If the world was fair, I think we'd both be somewhere without a bunch of old dogs hounding us for booze all the time. I swear, working at this place. I feel like I spend so much time listening to other people problems. You know what I need?"

"What's that?" Baxter asked attentively.

"I need a shrink. Someone that *I* get to talk to about all the shit I'm dealing with. I need to unravel after all the depraved trash I have to put up with here," Jade answered in a half-joking tone.

"You don't want a shrink," Baxter muttered.

"What do you mean, I don't want a shrink? I'd love one. I can't imagine having someone just sit there, letting me pour out all my problems onto them. I could just lay back in those big, expensive, leather couches they got. I don't imagine they'd mind if I had a beer while I spoke with 'em."

"They won't solve any of your problems; they just listen to them."

"That's fine with me. I'm not planning on solving any of the problems of my idiot customers that come in here complaining cause they hate their boss, or they got something from some girl, or some other trash like that. I mean, I know I'll never get one. Too expensive." She finished braiding her hair and began moving liquor bottles around the shelves, "But I s'pose that's how the world works: the rich get shrinks to keep them afloat when their sailboat starts sinking; us poor losers just drown."

"It's not all that bad," Baxter offered, "Is it?"

"Depends which day of the week it is," Jade responded with equal parts humor and resignation.

"Is there anything else you'd like from me?" the young man asked, standing next to the time cards.

"If you would just do a quick sweep of the sidewalk out front, then you can go. Thanks for the work today. Everything looks great."

"No problem, happy to do it," Baxter replied as he grabbed a broom and headed to the street.

The sidewalk in front of the bar was littered with broken glass and cigarette butts. It was rarely swept by The Toolbox staff as the establishment's clientele was more so the type to litter than to complain of it. Baxter looked up and down the street as he dutifully swept the sidewalk of refuse.

He wondered which direction Stretch generally came from to visit this part of town. The young man's sense of direction had been stunted with his upbringing in the orphanage, and he frequently struggled to navigate the streets of downtown effectively. Instead, he enjoyed a more aimless meander through the neighborhood streets and alleys. Stretch's departure from the bar caused a slight sense of anxiety in Baxter. The way he brought up drugs and money reminded the young man of his previous encounter with the ruffians outside of Stretch's modest abode. He also disliked that Stretch knew where he worked. It wasn't so much that he disliked Stretch's company, after all, in the multitude of ways his life was improving, his social life was extremely reclusive. It was the creeping anxiety that gnawed at the young man whenever he thought about disappointing his mentor, Sansarev. The way his young adult life had played out since arriving at St. Joseph's occasionally left him with a feeling of hopelessness for his future. He justified his use of recreational drugs as a special gift that he deserved for the hardships he'd been through. Of course other people shouldn't be using them, he thought, but his life was different. He'd been through so much; the drugs were necessary for him to stay afloat. Though Jade seemed sold on the idea of a shrink, Baxter had been down that road, and he still wasn't sure just how much damage it had caused.

After Baxter finished sweeping the sidewalk, he bid Jade farewell, and headed home for the evening. He hadn't noticed any traces of Stretch on his short walk home, but he paused before entering his building out of concern that Stretch could possibly discover where he resided. He didn't think his new companion had any malintent, but his beating at the hands of Stretch's associates left him with a quiet fear and a propensity to periodically glance over his shoulder.

21

A SOCIAL RENAISSANCE

Having spent his entire adult life in various types of captivity, Baxter had become an expert in the ways one's mind can be caged. He'd been caged by sorrow after the loss of his parents, caged in remorse after the orphanage, quite literally caged in jail and at Hothrest, and finally, socioeconomically caged in his derelict lean-to under the bridge outside Morristown. If there was a way to be immured, Baxter had lived through it. But now, with his own modest studio and a job down the street, for the first time in his life, he felt his level of freedom incredibly fulfilling. He was most surprised by how much he loved work. He took doubles at The Toolbox whenever he could and felt a deep satisfaction at the respect he earned from Jade and the regular rabble of the dive. As the week passed, and he anxiously awaited Sansarev's return visit, he worked to ensure the next time his old housemaster showed up, he'd be proud. He rid his apartment of any narcotic paraphernalia, cleaned up the place as best he could, and even salvaged some decor from The Toolbox that Jade had thrown out.

When Sansarev arrived the following weekend, he welcomed his mentor back to his apartment with a proud grin. "My boy, you look happy, and that makes me happy," Sansarev laughed gleefully as he entered. Baxter attempted to close the door behind the Russian, but Sansarev grabbed the door and his smile widened. "Remember when I told you I was bringing you surprises today?"

"Yeah, kinda," Baxter responded vaguely.

"Well, I did," the housemaster replied as he repeatedly snapped his fingers down the empty corridor. A pair of footsteps could be heard pattering down the hallway, and Baxter grew tense at who they could belong to. There weren't many people in his life that he felt comfortable having visit him at home, and he wasn't sure if he trusted Sansarev to differentiate between welcomed surprises and awkwardly tolerated guests. Luckily for everyone, Baxter's eyes widened when Max and Eliza stepped into the doorway of his apartment.

At first, Baxter was frozen in place, unable to speak, and unable to move. He was equally overjoyed and overwhelmed. Eventually, when he regained a touch of composure, he energetically embraced Max, and his old orphan cohort reciprocated gladly. He turned to Eliza, and though he dared not touch her, he smiled meekly and offered, "It's really good to see you, Eliza. I'm..." he hesitated, searching for the right thing to say, "I'm happy you're here."

"We had to drop in and see how you're doing," Max quickly responded as both Baxter and Eliza looked as though the meeting had the possibility of being uncomfortable. "From what we've heard, you've had a pretty wild time since I last saw you."

"At Hothrest," Baxter replied ruefully.

"Yeah..." Max trailed off. "Bet you're happy to be out of there, right?"

"Very," answered Baxter.

"Why don't we have a seat," Sansarev offered to the group. "I also brought us some lunch from Alejandra. I think you'd all like to know how happy she was to hear about this little rendezvous."

"I do miss Alejandra so much," Eliza said, happy to be able to join the conversation in an innocuous manner. "She was always so wonderful."

"She's always been a pillar of St. Joseph's," Sansarev added. "I know I certainly couldn't survive without her."

Max laughed, "Come on, Sansarev. You're too hard on yourself."

"You've never had my cooking," the Russian replied with an impish smirk.

"I have!" Eliza exclaimed. "Alejandra is definitely necessary."

"That was my kasha!" Sansarev bellowed with sincere

discouragement. "I always thought my kasha was excellent. I've always liked it..."

The three orphans exchanged sympathetic glances at each other and their old housemaster before breaking out in a bout of simultaneous snickering.

The apartment meeting was a surreal moment for each of the orphans. Baxter, of course, was still in shock that he was sitting in his apartment next to Eliza. He wanted to bring up that he felt like he could be dreaming, but quickly shot down that idea as their history may have made the comment less comical than intended. Eliza's perception of the rendezvous was noticeably less overwhelming than Baxter's; after all, she'd known ahead of time that the meeting would occur. Max was also slightly awkward in the meeting as he knew his old friend was completely unaware that he and Eliza had actually began a romantic engagement of their own. Baxter didn't know, and Max hadn't found an appropriate time to tell him. Sansarev was aware of the relationship, but when confided in by Max about the romance, he also concluded that Baxter might not be in the right emotional mindset to handle the news gracefully.

"What are you doing nowadays, Max?" Baxter asked, anxious to make conversation as if there was no sordid past to confront.

"I'm an apprentice steamfitter in the Builder's Guild," Max responded with pride, "It's hard work on the back, but the money is good."

"It's good work for a young man," Sansarev stated

encouragingly. "Young men need hard work; it puts them in touch with their ancestors."

"Their ancestors?" Max joked. "I don't know about all that, but like I said, the money is real good."

"You were such a bookworm at Joseph's. I figured you'd be working as a librarian," Baxter teased.

"He's still a bookworm," Eliza giggled.

"Just because I enjoy reading literature doesn't make me a bookworm," Max defended himself while elbowing Sansarev in the arm, "These barbarians... am I right?"

Sansarev laughed as he opened the basket full of the freshly made barbecoa tortas that Alejandra had kindly provided for them. Along with the sandwiches, she had added a small note to the basket that Sansarev happily read to his old wards:

> *Baxter, Max, and my dear, sweet Eliza,*
>
> *Nothing has made me happier in the past week then thinking that the three of you would spend time together again. I still remember watching you kids run through the gardens without a care in the world. Orphans always have difficult journeys, but I'm so very proud of what each of you has become, and the mountains you've climbed.*
> *Con amor,*
> *Alejandra*

When Sansarev finished the main part of the message, he wrinkled his nose at Alejandra's post scriptum, however, with further coaxing from Max, he read the rest, "P.S. Sergei apologizes ahead of time because the barbecoa makes him gassy."

"Yes!" Max shouted, "That's awesome."

"Gross," Eliza interjected.

The orphans all shared a good laugh at the their housemaster's expense as he adopted a rubicund hue of embarrassment. Sansarev chortled, "That only really happened once."

"If she thought to include it in the note, I'm sure it happened more than once, sir," Max replied. "They don't have barbecoa in Russia, right?"

Sansarev rolled his eyes with a playful smile and changed the subject, "Anyways, I brought you three together, not only because this reunion was past due, but I also believe you could all benefit from some friendly support. Baxter has picked up some unhealthy habits while living alone. No doubt a product of limited friendships."

Baxter shuffled his feet uncomfortably. He certainly wasn't prepared for Sansarev to air any of his dirty laundry to Max, and more importantly, Eliza. "Hey, I work; I've got an apartment," he responded with levity, "I think I'm doing okay."

"You most certainly are," responded Sansarev, "But you could be better, and I think you'd agree with that. Aren't you happy to see your friends again?"

"Of course!" Baxter exclaimed quickly. He was thrilled to see Max and Eliza and desperately wanted to rekindle a relationship with them both.

"Well, we've been through a lot together," Max proffered. "It makes sense that we're still around to help each other out. It's always helpful to have friends."

Baxter felt unfairly judged by Sansarev, and he didn't care to discuss what he considered infrequent drug experimentation with them. "*What did they know*," he thought. They'd both been through their own struggles, some of which he was painfully aware of, but their struggles hadn't been *his* struggles. Drugs, medications, narcotics, whatever you wished to call them, had been ubiquitous in his life after St. Joseph's. The very objects that Sansarev was so vehemently against were forced upon the young man during his tenure at Hothrest. He understood there was a difference, but he didn't necessarily agree with the degree of vitriol that was aimed at them. In many ways, he saw the pills he took at Hothrest as having similar effects to the pipe he'd smoked with Stretch. Almost as though the circumstances of the interaction were the criminal and not the drugs themselves. Regardless of his thoughts on the topic, he knew this wasn't the time for an argument, and he remained silent on his contention. "I'm just so excited to see you guys. Things have been so much better for me recently then they've been in the past. I'm really happy with the way things are going."

Sansarev kept a judicious eye on the young man but chose not to serve as the storm cloud on the boy's recently found contentment. "We're all pulling for you Mr. Bishop," he smiled.

Eliza chose to keep quiet through most of the

conversation. She had agreed to come with Max as moral support for her old orphanage mate, but she couldn't quell the gnawing resentment of her past with Baxter. On top of the awkward bitterness, she felt increasingly uncomfortable with the secretive nature of her new relationship with Max. Either way, she decided to be as cordial and affable as possible. "I think we're all doing well, considering where we came from," she offered warmly. "We've overcome a lot."

"Amen," Sansarev agreed, "And as it is with life, I'm sure we each have much more we'll have to overcome. And we'll have to do it with clear minds," he added, making eye contact with Baxter.

As the small talk continued, the four companions happily consumed Alejandra's fresh tortas and reminisced about better times from their past. They recalled the verdant gardens of St. Joseph's, the patter of orphan footsteps throughout the old home, and even the roguish pranks of their old friend, Seth.

"How's Seth doing with that older gentleman that adopted him?" Max asked.

"Last I heard, everything was going well. I received a letter from Seth about a month ago. Maybe two," the Russian responded between bites of his torta. "Did you know he was a hemophiliac?"

"Hemophiliac?" asked Baxter.

Sansarev swallowed his bite, wiped a strand of barbecoa from his mouth, and cleared his throat, "Someone whose blood doesn't properly clot. They can't stop bleeding."

"Wow, that sounds terrible," commented Eliza.

"No question. I found it an incredibly bizarre condition for a carpenter to have. One errant swing of the hammer, or a misguided saw blade, and you have a real catastrophe. He must be incredibly skilled," Sansarev spoke as he chewed. A life lived with orphans hadn't polished the Russian's table manners, and once out of the watchful eye of Alejandra, he became as gauche at the meal table as his children.

"Or incredibly stupid," Baxter quipped.

"Our passions and our circumstances don't always cooperate, Mr. Bishop," the housemaster warned, "Compromise and perseverance can turn adversaries into aides. I hope you all know that by now," he spoke with a solemn tone and made eye contact with each of his children. "You've all been through too much adversity to misunderstand how much it shapes who you are."

"I think we understand that," Max replied. "It's just confusing sometimes when you have so much regret over something that is so much a part of you. I'd love to have my family back. I think I'd be happier if I had them. I don't think I'd be who I am right now, but I think I'd be happier."

"That's true," Sansarev responded. "There will always be a void where they once were, but there's no filling that hole. I think those holes are the fountainhead of our compassion and empathy. You will forever have a greater capacity to understand the pain of others because of that hole. Would you be happier? I think most certainly. Would you be a better human being? I don't think so, and I think that's where the beauty of adversity comes into play. It helps you relate to the sadness of others. It makes you a more empathetic being."

"Are you happy you were an orphan?" Eliza questioned as she meticulously braided her long blonde hair.

"Happy?" Sansarev chuckled. "What is happiness?"

Eliza's casual smile melted into a more confounded expression as she pondered the question. "Happiness is... I don't know. It seems simple, but I know it's not. Happiness is surviving I guess. It's learning to appreciate every day. Ugh, I sound so cheesy," the girl blushed with embarrassment. "I shouldn't have said anything."

Baxter immediately interjected to support his old flame, "I don't think it's cheesy at all. I think that's exactly what happiness is." Although Baxter's words were supportive of the young lady, his tone carried a false enthusiasm that came off to everyone like a vapid agreement based on attraction, not one of true philosophical consensus. "I mean, all we can do is survive, right?"

"I think everyone has a different idea of real happiness," Max offered in an attempt to dispel Baxter's chivalrous engagement with Eliza. "It depends on what you've been through and what you want to accomplish. We've been through a lot, so I think we have lower expectations than others. I know I just appreciate being around the people I care about; taking care of 'em." He smiled at Eliza first before offering his grin to Sansarev and Baxter.

"Well put, Max. You've always had a way with words,"

the Russian chuckled. "At St. Joseph's, I always tried to keep my children social. It's so easy to isolate yourself and avoid others when you're dealing with the melancholy that frequently comes paired with orphans. Companionship has always struck me as one of the surest paths to lasting happiness. We're incredibly social creatures, after all. Which is also why I wanted this reunion." Sansarev's gaze became sympathetic as it rested on Baxter. "I've told Max and Eliza about your drug use, Mr. Bishop. I'm sure you're upset with me for doing so, as I have no doubt you've rationalized your new habits, but I can't stand idly by while you venture down a path that I know is riddled with such pain."

Baxter's own countenance quickly darkened at what he felt was a misrepresentation of his world. His lips melted into a frown as he addressed his housemaster, "For as long as I can remember my life has always been pain. No one complained when I was given drugs every day at Hothrest. *Every day.*"

"I'm sure you know how that is completely different, Mr. Bishop," Sansarev answered.

"Is it *completely* different?" Baxter countered. "There are obviously differences, but I see more similarities than you do. Everyone wants to believe they know what's going on in my head. Even if I disagree, they seem to know better than me. Do you know what it's like constantly having people tell you that the way you feel is wrong? Even though they don't really know how you feel?" Baxter pointed at the floor where Sansarev had first noticed the pipe that

Stretch had given him, "What if that made me feel better? What if it gave me hope?"

"Don't be ridiculous, Mr. Bishop. If you believe hope can come from poison, you've learned little from your trials," the Russian sneered. "Counting on these mind numbing drugs to heal you is an addiction to toxic bandaids. Nothing more. Hope doesn't truly come from these fickle remedies-"

"I think it's easy to point out what doesn't bring hope. At this point, nothing has brought lasting hope. Everything is a bandaid. You pointing it out doesn't change anything. It doesn't prove anything except you don't understand how much bandaids can help," Baxter returned defensively. "I'm so tired of adults knowing what hurts but offering no real help on how to feel better. I took advice from adults and went through therapy-" he hesitated, remembering that Eliza was present but quickly continued, "And it didn't give me hope. I took drugs at Hothrest and had more therapy, and again, none of it helped. You want to know what doesn't help? People assuming they know how much damage has been done and believing my situation is similar to their's. Have you ever thought that my pain is greater than your's ever was? That the things that helped you; the advice that you have to give, is based on a lesser pain and won't help me?" Baxter's eyes began to mist up as his frustration mounted, and he frantically wiped a tear away as he buried his face in his hands.

Sansarev and Eliza exchanged concerned glances with one another as Max reached out a hand and gently patted

Baxter's back. He cleared his throat and spoke with a quiet, soothing tone, "We can't empathize with your pain, Bax. We all know that. What you've been through-" Max smiled and whistled, "None of us can really know what's going on with you. We just don't want you doing more damage to yourself than what's already been done. I can't imagine living at an asylum. It had to be Hell. I can't say I wouldn't be doing the same thing if I was in your position, but it's not hard to look around at people who have gone down the path you're talking about and seeing where it took them. I've spent time downtown; I've seen the people yelling at parked cars, living in boxes, roaming the sidewalks for their next fix. I'm not that worried that you've done it a time or two to try and escape. I'm worried you're going to continue using to escape. I'm only afraid for you because of how much I can understand the desire to relieve the pain."

Eliza wanted to say something but remained silent. She hated herself for being unable to comfort the young man, but simply having Baxter present resurrected memories and emotions that she had spent years working to bury. To see the source of so much of her pain being crippled by its own anguish was a profound experience for the girl. It was the first time she was able to understand the psychological depths of Baxter's wounds. She knew she'd never be able to forget but witnessing her old friend's devastation encouraged the possibility of forgiveness.

"Do you really think drugs will help you in the long run?" Max asked with sincerity. "Where do you see evidence of them helping other people?"

Baxter kept his head lowered for a moment before lifting his face and wiping his eyes. "I think that's what people don't understand. I don't think anyone's doing drugs to fix their problems; they're doing drugs to escape their problems. I don't think they're going to fix me," Baxter conceded. "But eventually you reach the point where you don't think anything can. People tell you that they're not what you should be doing. They say drugs won't fix you, but they're answering a question that no one ever asked. What would you say if I asked you how to fix myself? How do I escape my parents' death? And not just the memory of finding my mother lying in a pool of her own blood, but how do I live, knowing I'll never see them again. How do I live with that?" Tears rolled down Baxter's eyes, and he furiously wiped them from his face with the sleeve of his shirt. "How about St. Joseph's!?" he shouted, becoming even more unhinged. "I'm sorry, Eliza! I'm so sorry. I never-" he gasped for breath as his emotions overwhelmed him.

Eliza remained still. Furious at herself for being unable to console him, but powerless within her profound ambivalence. Her nature had always been one of sympathy and compassion, but her mind was paralyzed with toxic remembrances.

Max also froze. He was torn between protecting Eliza and allowing Baxter to voice his sorrow. Max hoped the apology may serve to exorcise the demons that haunted his old friend.

"I never meant to hurt you," Baxter whimpered again. "How about Hothrest? How about nightmares ... straitjackets ... drugs ... cells? How about hurting people you love? How about not knowing what's real anymore ..." He trailed off, and his eyes listlessly gazed off into an unseen horizon. He sat in silent stillness for several seconds with his eyes locked in vacant disassociation. Each of his companions remained motionless, certain that something needed to be said, but unsure of what words could permeate the boy's catatonia. Baxter's eyes didn't wake from his dissociative episode until Eliza gently place her hand on his knee.

"There's nothing anyone can say to fix the past, Baxter. *We* know that. But you won't heal until you forgive yourself," Eliza coaxed as her own eyes began showing traces of tears. "I ... hated you, for so long," she sobbed. "I couldn't understand why it happened to me. I didn't understand what I'd done to deserve it. I had to learn that there's no big plan. It's not a question of deserving or undeserving. Terrible things happen. They just happen, and we have to get over them. The terrible things we hold onto steal from us. They steal what's good and amplify what's bad. You have to let go, Baxter. If you don't, they'll destroy you."

"How do you know I'm not already destroyed?"

"Because you're here. You're alive. And as long as we're living, we have to fight sadness," Eliza responded.

"Existence is suffering," muttered Sansarev.

Baxter attempted a weak smile at his friends. He sincerely appreciated their concerns, and he knew their cajoling came from the best of intentions. "I'm trying, you guys. I promise."

"We know you are, Bax," Max replied with a more up-beat tone. "We're just here to help however we can."

"Thanks," Baxter answered. "One day the pain will all be over, and I can't wait."

Sansarev and Max exchanged nervous glances at the young man's eerie comment as they cleaned up from lunch.

"We have to bounce, Bax," Max said as he washed his hands, "But we'll be back soon. Make sure you take care of yourself and try to keep your head up."

"Thanks so much for coming, you guys," Baxter replied, "It means everything to me."

The three visitors exchanged embraces with their imperiled companion and departed the flat. Baxter quietly looked out the window at the apartments next door, watching various neighbors mill about like ants busily occupied by their own joys and sorrows.

"Existence is suffering," Baxter repeated under his breath as he traversed his modest apartment and closed the door behind them.

22

ROUND TWO

Baxter appreciated the concern and support of his friends, but even with their sincere affections, he felt an unfortunate distance from them as if the obstacles within his own life had lessened his ability to relate. Max couldn't understand. His hurdles didn't compare to Baxter's, not really. Eliza had been through a difficult time; he couldn't deny that, but his world felt infinitely darker. She hadn't been the target of malice the way he had. Even Sansarev, in all of his profound wisdom, seemed ill-equipped to comprehend the severity of the young man's psychological wounds, and as hard as Baxter tried to downplay his past, he always returned to his most deeply held fear, that he was irreparable.

Over the next week, Baxter kept to a strict schedule. He'd finish his shifts at The Toolbox and immediately return home to his apartment. It wasn't that he was afraid of running into Stretch, but he reluctantly admitted to himself the appeal of the drugs. He understood they were a bandaid, a temporary measure to assuage his trauma, but even those ephemeral episodes of solace seemed a gift of mercy. He did what he could during his leisure time to keep his mind from dwelling on his haunting past, but despite his best intentions, he couldn't shrug off the melancholy that accompanied recollections of his parents and Eliza. Seeing her again had been more difficult than he'd anticipated. He still found her to be strikingly beautiful, but her disposition towards him wasn't the amorous spirit she displayed in his dreams. She was a real person with authentic sorrow, and despite his ardent hopes that she'd forget the sins he'd committed, her kindness to him seemed to emanate from behind a veil of practiced detachment. She was too kind to be overtly rude but too hurt to be authentically kind, and it furthered the young man's frustration with his present situation.

Eliza had returned to his life, though it didn't seem she particularly wished to be there. He'd uncovered information regarding the murder of his parents, but the individuals who he believed had some role in the tragedy seemed untouchable to law enforcement. It was a reality worthy of Sisyphus, full of developments, that in the grand scheme of things, accomplished nothing.

It was the Friday after his visit with his old orphanage mates, and Jade had demanded Baxter take the day off.

The young man didn't want any days off as he found free time to be more disconcerting than his shifts at the bar, but he acquiesced to her demands of a brief sabbatical and spent the day cleaning up his apartment. Although he didn't blame Sansarev for keeping the arrival of Max and Eliza secret, his apartment had sadly been a mess, and he hoped they'd return after a thorough cleaning.

"So your girl's back in the picture, kid?" Cassius questioned as he looked out the window into the neighboring apartments.

"She's not my girl," Baxter responded coldly. He wasn't particularly in the mood to deal with Cassius' brand of upbeat ridicule; however, he was at least in some part happy that he had company.

"I'm pretty sure she is. I mean, you might not be her man, but she's definitely your girl, am I right?" Cassius teased with a toothy grin.

"Neither of us are each other's anythings," the young man rebuked testily. "We liked each other when we were younger, and life took us different ways. We're still friends."

"I don't know, man," Cassius replied with a snicker. "Seems to me like your everyone's charity case. Everyone walkin' on eggshells 'round you. Everyone trying to protect Little-Boy-Baxter. Don't you get tired of being the victim?"

"I'm not the victim," Baxter growled menacingly at Cassius, but even as he refuted his old friend's criticism, he knew there was an aggravating amount of truth to the words. "I didn't ask for anyone's sympathy or pity. I'm taking care of myself, and I'd say I'm doing a damn good job of it."

"Hiding from the police, dumpster diving for food, and getting high with strangers?" Cassius mocked sardonically, "Yeah buddy, I'd say you're living the dream."

"Fuck the police," Baxter spat. "They can't do anything to the people that hurt my parents, but they're dead set on finding me. As if I'm doing anything to anyone."

"Well, you know why they're after you. Just because your girl seems to forgive ya doesn't mean the state will. How long are you gonna hide out here? Running between your job at that dive and your apartment? Ya know they'll find ya eventually, right?"

Baxter rubbed his head, exhausted from Cassius' interrogation and frustrated by the authentic obstacles his friend brought up. The conversation further darkened Baxter's mood. He hated the veracity of Cassius' comments. He'd viewed his progress since Hothrest as something to be proud of. He'd held down a job, maintained his apartment, and developed a couple new friendships, but he resented his friends portraying him as a pitiable drug addict. He refused more drugs than they'd ever been offered. He'd found something that relaxed him temporarily and had never abused it to a reckless degree. "I'm fine, Cassius. I wish everyone would mind their own business." Baxter angrily threw some laundry across the room as he opened the door. "I'm outta here. I need to get some fresh air."

"Be careful out there, kid. You know better than anyone, that world can eat you up."

As Baxter stepped out of the front lobby, he admired his building in the orange glow of the setting sun. Evening had arrived in downtown Morristown, and a section of town that was generally viewed as distressed and rundown was granted a sliver of elegance from the sun's final visitation for the day. The young man took a deep breath as he crossed the street and headed away from The Toolbox. He didn't wish to be recognized so he stuck to avenues alien to his normal routes. Although he'd lived in the neighborhood for some time now, he'd avoided exploring the surrounding streets. Unfamiliar alleyways held a debilitating fear for him. He could still remember the ruffians who'd blocked him into the dead end alley and mercilessly assaulted him. The memory caused him to grit his teeth and gently slide his fingers down his ribcage, remembering the pain that had left him helpless and terrified after the mugging outside Stretch's.

Tonight, he wished to simply clear his mind. The rendezvous with Eliza and Max left him feeling ambivalent concerning his friends. On one hand, he still clearly carried feelings for Eliza. He was uncertain whether her reserved demeanor at the impromptu brunch was because she no longer held him in an affectionate regard or if the traumatic wound that he'd inflicted on her simply hadn't fully healed. He contemplated whether or not her wounds were similar to his, and in that case, would she ever heal? Would he? It was a supremely disconcerting thought for the boy which led him to his other aggravating conundrum. Both Sansarev and Max had been quick to demonize his narcotic use, but what if Eliza was the only one who could empathize with his need to escape. He didn't disagree with Sansarev's characterization of drugs as an escape; he was simply skeptical of either Sansarev or Max's need to run away.

The sun had finished its descent, and the streetlights all weakly pulsed as they warmed up for their graveyard shift, illuminating the shadowy pockets of the poorly kept boulevard. Baxter had wandered a fair distance from the safety of Stonegate but was enjoying his time outside the confines of his cramped apartment. It felt good to stretch his legs and take in the fresh evening air. Whenever he passed by one of the bars or restaurants, he'd glance in through the street windows to see the customers enjoying their carefree existences. He always tried his best not to sneer at the fortunate, but occasionally his self-pity would surface, and he'd be unable to help but scowl at the undeserved luck of the jovial revelers. After a few moments continuing down the tenebrous avenue, he decided it would be safest to return home. He crossed the street and began his way back, looking into various closed shops to admire their wares. As he passed an alleyway, he heard some rustling emanate from a pile of garbage bags. He didn't wish to encounter anyone so he quickened his steps while looking over his shoulder to see if the source of the rustling had chosen to pursue him. Although the rustling eventually stopped, without looking where he was going, Baxter collided forcefully with another individual on the sidewalk.

"Sorry, I heard something in the alley over there and-"

"Well, holy shit!" shouted the stranger. "You!"

Baxter looked into the face of the individual he ran into, and his face melted into terror as he recognized one of the men that accosted him outside Stretch's apartment. He turned to run, but the young man tackled him to the ground.

"Oh shit, you're not going anywhere!" the gang member shouted as he continued to drive his shoulder into Baxter's gut. "You shouldn't have come back to Morristown. We're gonna bury your ass!"

"I'm just going home! Get off of me! Help!" Baxter angled his head towards the lit up restaurants only a block away at this point, but there was no sign of aid. He did notice three more boys turn from a nearby alley and begin running towards him. One of them he recognized from the beating, and he realized they were coming to assist his attacker. If they reached him, he had little hope to escape, and they'd probably be set on ensuring he didn't survive the beating. With a swift kick, Baxter was able to knock his assailant off him and into the display window of a retail store. The gang member struck the glass hard, causing the entire display case to shatter, and the store's alarm to go off. The high-pitched, loud alarm reverberated across the dark avenue and caused the customers of the nearby restaurants to slowly begin glancing outside to witness the young men sprinting down the street. Baxter seized the opportunity, jumped to his feet, and dashed in the opposite direction of his assailants.

Baxter cut corners and raced down side streets, but one of the young men chasing him was significantly faster. Eventually, the faster assailant caught him and grabbed him by the shirt, but Baxter spun around and desperately lunged at his assaulter. The attacker was caught off guard, lost his balance, and ended up hitting the ground with Baxter on top of him. A short scuffle ensued, but Baxter was well aware the other boys would be on top of him shortly. He grabbed his opponent's jacket and attempted to sling him to the ground, but the jacket tore off in Baxter's hands and both were catapulted to opposite sides of the alley. Baxter sprung up from the filthy ground with ripped jacket in hand and attempted to flee the alleyway, but it was too late. The gang members had surrounded the alley and a couple of the men stood guard at the exits. Baxter spun around in the alley, running his hands through piles of trash for anything he could use as a makeshift weapon, but all he found was a discarded serving tray. As the men slowly closed in on him, he swung the hard plastic tray furiously in order to fend them off.

"This shit is adorable," one of the men said. "You guys see this? He's stole Mick's jacket?

"Din't anyone teach you stealin's wrong?" another of the assailants snickered.

"Looks like we gonna need to teach this boy some discipline," the first man replied with a sinister smile. "This gonna hurt you a whole helluva lot more than it's gonna hurt us."

Baxter backed up against the wall and racked his mind for any possibility for escape. The exits were covered by two men each, and the attacker he had slung against the wall was back on his feet, slowly approaching him with a long knife in his right hand.

"That was my favorite jacket," the man said, brandishing his knife menacingly. "You tore my favorite jacket." He pointed the tip of his knife at Baxter's face, laughed, and growled, "I'm gonna slit your throat, skin you alive, and wear your skin to keep me warm, you little piece of shit."

23

OUT OF THE FRYING PAN
AND INTO THE FIRE

A s the man's knife slashed back and forth, slicing through the dark atmosphere, Baxter tripped backwards and fell against the cold, brick wall. The knife blade would occasionally flash with the reflection of orange streetlights as it whistled in front of Baxter. The man stabbed twice, missing his first attempt, but nicking Baxter's forearm with his second lunge. Baxter yelped in pain as the blade drew blood. The other gang members whistled and cheered their champion on as his smile grew with the sight of his opponent's fresh wound. Baxter couldn't believe this was happening again. His limbs were paralyzed with fear, and his heart pounded inside his chest like tribal drums. The attacker lashed out again, scoring another glancing cut in the orphan's bicep. Baxter cried out again and grabbed his arm. The blood from the wound seeped in between his fingertips and caused him to fall back helplessly against the wall of the alley. He whimpered in resignation as the other four men slowly surrounded him, smiling with realization that they were going to be able to end the boy's life.

"Freeze!" roared a voice from the mouth of the alley. "Give me a reason to put you assholes down!" barked the voice. A bright beam of light shot across the dingy alley and pinned itself on the face of the man with the knife. One of the attackers took another step closer to Baxter before the figure raised a handgun beside the flashlight and fired off a shot into a pile of garbage bags. At this point, the five men cussed aloud and quickly scrambled to escape the alleyway and the armed rival. One of the assailants slipped on some soggy leftovers from one of the nearby eateries and toppled into a pile of refuse, cussing profusely as he shook himself free from the discarded food. Eventually, he was able to claw himself out of the pile and continued to flee the alleyway, leaving his dignity behind with the used coffee grinds.

"This is officer six-three-seven. I've got five men running south down Mercy. Need units to engage," the figure barked into the radio.

It became clear to the young man that the gun aimed at his head was held by a cop, and he cussed his cowardice for being unable to retreat. He stayed pinned against the brick wall. He desperately wished to flee the scene as well, but he dared not follow his attackers nor take his chance heading towards the gun-wielding figure. His legs were stiff with fear, and the blood that was beginning to dry left his fingers feeling exceedingly filthy. He quickly wrapped the torn jacket around his arm to cover the the knife wound.

"Hands on your head! Face the wall!" the figure commanded.

He couldn't go back to jail, not now. Not after he'd done everything right.

"Turn around and put your hands against the wall or I'll put you down," growled the officer again. "You punk gangs need to be dealt with."

The young man complied with the request and slowly placed his hands against the brick wall, cursing his poor fortune. "I'm not one of them. They attacked me."

The light grew brighter on his face as the figure cautiously approached, "Just wandering around the alleyways at night, right?" the officer questioned with a mocking voice. "Make sure you keep those hands where I can see them."

"They attacked me. Please, I haven't done anything wrong," the young man pleaded.

The light grew brighter, and the officer's footsteps louder as both grew closer to the young man. Time crawled for the orphan as anxiety continued to climb from his stomach into his esophagus. He pressed his palms hard against the grungy alley wall and began to softly cry.

The officer grew closer with the light shining directly on the young man's face. After a long pause, the officer cleared its throat and spoke in a hard whisper, "Baxter?"

Baxter froze for a moment before he recognized the tenor of the voice, "Yes," he answered, still trembling.

"Oh my goodness, Baxter!" the officer whispered again. "It's me; it's Shabon."

Baxter slowly turned his head to see the officer who had now turned the light away from his face and cast it on her own. It was indeed his old friend Shabon Da'Brickashaw. He fell to his knees and gasped with relief. "Please, Shabon. You can't arrest me. They'll take me to jail. They'll never let me out; they'll throw away the key. I couldn't stay at Hothrest. I was getting worse there. I had to leave." The confessions poured from the young man like water from a busted levee, but he remained on his knees facing the alley wall.

"Baxter, what are you doing out here?" Shabon asked with genuine concern. "What are you doing around these hoodlums?"

"Th-they came after me earlier. Th-they thought I had drugs or money. They beat the Hell out of me m-m-months ago. I ran into them, and they recognized me and chased me back into this alleyway." Baxter's words stuttered and broke as his body trembled from the fear that was just now beginning to depart his shaking frame.

Two police cruisers with sirens blazing raced by the mouths of the alley in the direction of the fleeing gang members. The high-pitched whirring of the sirens echoed throughout the alleyway.

As the noise of the sirens dissipated down the dark boulevard, Shabon placed a gentle hand on his shoulder and continued to speak softly, "I can't believe you're here. You know they're looking for you everywhere. Gosh, baby, let me look at you." Baxter slowly turned from the alley wall and faced his old friend. She shined the light to the side to see his face without blinding him. "Honey, you look so different. You've grown up," she offered with a sympathetic tone. "But what are you doing here? Backup is on its way and they're going to take you in when they get here."

"I can't go back," the young man blurted out. "Please, Shabon, I can't go back. They'll never let me go. I'll never hurt anyone. I'll never do anything wrong."

Shabon was visibly torn. Her history with the young man left her confident in his good nature, but she wasn't in the habit of abandoning her duty. If news ever got out that she'd had Baxter Bishop in custody and let him go, she'd lose her job without question. Sadly, she also agreed with the boy that the incarceration that would follow this arrest was most certainly not in the best interest of the young man's welfare.

"Baxter..." she sighed.

"Please, Shabon. I'll stay inside for days. No one will know it was me. I'm part of the reason you guys are even going to catch those gang members. I was your bait. You'll get them because of me. Please, let me go," he sobbed breathlessly.

"Ugh," Shabon exhaled. "This is the stupidest thing I've ever done. Why do I care about you, honey? It was easier taking care of your ass when you were younger."

Without warning, Baxter lunged out and wrapped his arms around Shabon. "Thank you, Shabon; thank you so much!"

Shabon squeezed her old friend tight before prying herself free of his rigorous embrace. "Honey, you gotta get out of here. The next cars are gonna come to me, and they gonna expect you here. I'll tell 'em I didn't get a positive identification and that I was knocked down. It's gonna be an embarrassing story to hear at the station, but you gotta get out of here or you're gonna get caught."

Baxter didn't waste another second after his friend's command. He gathered himself, wiped some trash and grime off his clothes, and departed the alley, attempting to look as nonchalant as possible. Onlookers gave curious glances at first, but after seeing Shabon casually block off the alley, they all assumed the criminal activity had been resolved, and they could continue with the banality of their evening.

Baxter didn't look back as he walked down the side-walk. He exhaled sharply with relief as he made his way toward Stonegate; if there was one thing he'd learned, it was the danger of looking back.

24

THE IRREPARABLE

*"O God, I could be bounded in a nutshell
and count myself a king of infinite space,
were it not that I have bad dreams."*
- Hamlet -

W hen Baxter finally arrived back at Stonegate, he
carefully removed the jacket he'd torn from his
assailant. The knife wounds stung as he carefully slid the sleeves off his arms. The lacerations weren't
as deep as he'd thought, but the blood hadn't fully clotted
and still trickled from the cuts. He felt he knew a thing or
two about treating wounds after witnessing Alejandra treat
his injuries from his previous assault. He applied a bit of
soap to a clean rag and dabbed the wounds gently, gritting
his teeth from the pain. Afterwards, he tore an undershirt
in two and meticulously wrapped the cuts.

The young man felt perpetually trapped. Everywhere he turned and in every aspect of his life, he felt unable to escape. Even within his own mind, his thoughts seemed to rebel against him. He wasn't safe anywhere. He was equally hunted by those that meant him either harm or safety, and he felt certain that his life would be harmed by both sides. He sunk down onto his bed, drying his tears with the sleeve of the jacket when he felt a hard object in the jacket pocket. He rummaged through the jacket and removed a small pipe with a tiny clear plastic bag of crystals. The apparatus was identical to the one he'd used at Stretch's apartment. The young man immediately felt conflicted. He was in pain. He was scared. He felt exhausted but paradoxically unable to sleep. He could immediately create a dozen reasons why he felt justified in partaking, but in the back of his mind there was still the wise, nagging advice of Sansarev. He put the pipe down, turned off the lights, and rested his head on the pillow, welcoming anything to the forefront of his thoughts that would replace his desire to relieve his pain and trepidation through drugs.

He closed his eyes, prayed for sleep, and imagining the control he could finally assert on his life, if only he could dream. He longed for control. His dreams were now the only place he felt comfortable; the only place he felt safe. Despite his uncertainty and suspicion concerning Schaffer, he attempted the image rehearsal that she'd had taught him. He pictured himself running through the lush gardens of St. Joseph's with Seth and Max; he remembered watching Eliza splash crystal clear water out of the garden fountain, giggling as the sparkling droplets flashed in the sunlight. He reminisced about a time when his mother and father were simply part of a happy family. He attempted to return to a time when his life embraced the carefree spirit expected of childhood, but the corrupted present repeatedly contaminated his meditation. For the better part of an hour, he lay awake in bed, his mind oscillating between images of childhood innocence and the hellish events that had created his current dystopia. He kicked the sheets off and covered his face with his hands in frustration. He felt powerless to the conniving devils of his mind, and eventually, his better angels surrendered to hopelessness as he reached for the pipe at his bedside.

He placed some of the crystalline substance inside the glass bauble and gently inhaled, feeling the smoke seep into his lungs. He closed his eyes and allowed the chemicals to rearrange the fundamental tides of his mind. Joy, anguish, hope, fear, love, and pain all coalesced into an amalgamation of indiscernible fog. A haze that a healthy mind might conceive as a wasteful and impractical adaptation, but to Baxter's crippled psyche, it was a pause button, a reset switch, a mulligan. For the young man, the healthy mind had become a chimera. From St. Joseph's to Hothrest to Stonegate, his quest for a tranquil mind had failed and a deep, resentful, self-loathing had blossomed in the aftermath of failure. But the drugs blunted the psychological turmoil. Baxter rationalized the use of the narcotic as a medicine to treat the often misunderstood maladies of the mind, like a simple tablet of ibuprofen for a sprain. He took another hit from the pipe and held the breath for several seconds before blowing out another billowing cloud of smoke. He felt his head sink further into the pillow, and his lips curled into the familiar smile he recalled from Stretch's apartment. He closed his eyes and before long felt himself departing for a new world.

25

A RUDE AWAKENING

"**O**h my god, Baxter!"
"Wake up, man!"
"Baxter!? Baxter!?"

As he opened his eyes, the world was unusually blurry to Baxter, as if his mind having reset, required a brief period to calibrate itself to the multitude of new stimuli.

"What the hell are you doing, man?" Max asked sternly. As his figure came into greater focus, Baxter recognized the pipe and bag next to his hands. "This stuff will kill you. Do you not believe us? Or do you just not care?"

"Max-," Eliza spoke calmly, trying to de-escalate the situation.

"No, no, no," Max barked back, interrupting the girl, "Everyone's always on eggshells around him. Maybe that's the problem. I know what you're going to say. We don't understand. Maybe we *do* understand. Maybe we need to stop tip-toeing around the room and talk about how we really feel instead of sugar-coating everything and molly-coddling him."

"You're an idiot if you think his life has been sugar-coated," she answered sharply.

"I didn't mean his life-" Max backpedalled. "I just mean the way everyone treats him after a catastrophe strikes, like it wasn't his..." Max's voice faded before he could finish his sentence. He could detect an anger growing in his mind that he wasn't sure was entirely justifiable.

Baxter was still groggily acclimating to being awake while simultaneously coming down from the drug's high. He lifted his head off the pillow and reached down to rub his aching arm.

"He's bleeding!" Eliza exclaimed with shock.

"What happened, Bax?" Max asked. "Looks pretty bad."

Baxter coughed and sat up in his bed, "It's nothing. Much better than it could've been. What are you guys doing here? How'd you get in?"

"We came to surprise you and take you out to breakfast," Eliza answered.

"You didn't answer when we knocked, and the door was unlocked so we just came in," Max added. "Makes sense that you didn't answer. You were high."

Baxter glared at Max, "I wish I was high. Right now, I'm not, and my arm is killing me."

"What happened?" repeated Eliza, becoming frustrated that such a seemingly important question was being avoided.

"Nothing," Baxter replied with a surly tone. "Just more of my sugar-coated life."

"That's not what I meant," Max replied defensively. "Just that people are scared of saying some stuff to you."

"I don't blame them. I have pretty terrible thoughts about most things I hear people saying about me," Baxter commented as he carefully removed the torn pieces of undershirt from his wounds. "Not really interested in breakfast though."

"You need to talk to Sansarev," Max offered. "He needs to know whatever is going on."

"Oh yeah?" Baxter laughed cynically, "And what exactly is Sansarev going to do to help me?"

"He'll-" Max began to reply before his voice faded into uncertainty. "He'll have some type of advice. He got you this place, didn't he?"

"He paid for the first month. I've been working and paying for everything since then."

"He cares about you, Bax," Max continued. "We all do."

"I know you do; I know you do. It just doesn't help me much, and I'm tired of people thinking it does. As though good intentions actually do something."

"What can do we do to help?" Eliza asked.

Baxter paused. The question felt bizarre to him, and he wasn't sure why. "I don't know anymore. I feel like at one point I would've known, but I don't anymore. Sometimes I feel like it's just too late for me. Too much damage has been done. I'm broken, and I can't be fixed."

"Is that why you're convinced you need drugs?" Max pressed him.

"I don't think I need drugs. I don't think they're fixing me. In fact, I'm pretty sure they're doing damage, but I don't care anymore," Baxter responded with a listless look out the apartment window. "I don't know how much longer I have."

"Baxter! Don't say things like that," Eliza gasped. "You're just a kid. You have so much time in front of you."

"I know I'm a kid, and I know I have a lot of time ahead of me. I just don't think I want it."

"Don't say that!" Eliza repeated.

"I don't think living my life is worth it. I think there's more pain then the brief segments of happiness are worth," he responded, still looking out the windows.

"You just need a fresh start," Max replied with a forced chuckle in an attempt to bring some levity to the conversation.

"That's an easy thing to say, Max," Baxter responded with a glare. "If I'm caught by the police, I go to jail. If I'm caught by that gang, I honestly think they'll kill me. So what? Being outside my apartment is off limits? What exactly do you suggest I do with this fresh start?"

Max was silent. He didn't have an answer. He couldn't agree with his friend that suicide was an option, but he recognized his inability to empathize with Baxter's trauma. He knew his friend had been through Hell. He sincerely believed suicide was a terrible course of action, but he struggled to prove that to someone with Baxter's tragic history. "Look Bax," Max spoke softly, "Just let me talk to Sansarev. He'll know what to do."

"Oh yeah?" Baxter replied meekly.

"Just do me a favor, man."

"What's that?"

"No more drugs. I get that they feel good now, but you said yourself. You think they're hurting you. Just hold off on them until we have a better idea on how to help. And I promise man, Liza and I will come back and visit you. Frequently, I promise. Deal?"

It was Baxter's turn to remain silent.

"Deal?" Eliza pushed him.

Baxter looked up at her. Her eyes were beautiful, but inside their beauty was an expression of profound pity that reminded Baxter that she saw a broken man. He wasn't worthy of her love anymore and that realization cut deeper than any knife. Her eyes used to contain admiration; she'd even desired him, but those empyrean constellations had left the celestial azure of her eyes. He looked at her supple lips, but they no longer conferred desire, only shame, pitiful shame.

"Deal," Baxter muttered breathlessly as a tear slid down his cheek. He had lost her. He finally acknowledged that, and he couldn't wait to end it all.

26

STRAY LAW DOGS

*"It is sometimes an appropriate
response to reality to go insane."*
- Philip K. Dick -

Max and Eliza departed as swiftly as they'd arrived once Baxter promised to stop his drug use. Max had taken his paraphernalia as a safeguard which left Baxter in an empty room without companionship and without his self-prescribed medicine. He lay inert on his bed in a deep melancholy, studying the apartments that he'd once watched for the bustling activity of his neighbors. He remembered the attractive girl he'd admired from across the gap, always hoping he'd run into her outside the building and strike up an engaging conversation. He now imagined the same look in her eyes as he'd seen in Eliza's gaze. The look of pity. It felt like disgust without the repulsion, as though they didn't mean to offend and had the best intentions, but still found nothing of real value in their subject. The young man wondered if this is what depression was: the slow and complete dissolution of one's self-esteem, to wake up in the morning and find yourself completely valueless and with no conceivable hope of acquiring any true value again. He felt as though the only emotion the future could hold was simply waiting for it all to end. There was a wide chasm that sat between him and hope, and there was no way across the gaping pit.

When he heard an authoritative knock on the door, his first thought was that his orphan cohorts were certainly planning on keeping their promise of *frequent* visits, but upon opening the door, he was startled to find Shabon Da'Brickashaw and Detective Caine standing in the corridor.

Caine smiled at the young man and doffed an unmarked baseball cap, "So this is where you're hiding."

"We spoke to Sansarev," Shabon interjected, reading the young man's thoughts. "He told us where you were, and we need your help."

"I-my help?" Baxter stuttered in shock. "You need my help? With what? Are you arresting me?"

Caine was the first to laugh, "Everyone keeps asking me that question. Look kid, you're not on my caseload, and from everything I know about you, you're not much of a danger to the general public. Your parents however? They *are* on my caseload, and we're spinning our wheels trying to land real evidence. I understand you've been avoiding me, and you had good reason to. Hell, if I was in your situation, I'd be doing the exact same thing," he remarked with a smile. He poked his head in the doorframe and briefly glanced around the spartan apartment before commenting, "Eh, I'd probably decorate a little bit better, ya know? Make the hideaway a bit more homey. But that's just me, maybe you've gotten into a more austere lifestyle."

"Funny, Jimmy," Shabon chuckled. "We're not here to arrest you, Baxter. We just want to find out if you know anything that could help us, anything that could help you. We want to find out what happened to your parents and hold those people responsible."

Baxter paused in his doorway. He trusted Shabon completely and realized he had no power in this situation. If he declined to help, he'd just be arrested so he decided to step aside and welcome the two officers into his humble home.

Shabon was significantly more gracious with her praise of the young man's home. "Baxter, this looks fantastic, baby! You've really set yourself up a cozy little nook. It smells kind-"

"It smells terrible in here, bud," Caine lightly chuckled.

"I was going to say it smells like a young man, but I think cracking these windows would be a great start," Shabon stated as she traversed the apartment and lifted a stubborn window.

"Guess you don't have many visitors," Caine joked as he searched the apartment for a chair. "Bah, the floor's good enough for me. Have a seat, buddy. We don't want to take up too much of your time, but we're trying to climb a greased pole down there at the station concerning your ma and pop."

"Climb a greased pole?" Baxter questioned with a confused look.

"Yeah, Sansarev informed us that you're up to date on your old therapist, Schaffer, and Fenway," Caine said, removing a small notepad from his breast pocket. "Climb a greased pole, ya know? Spinning our wheels. We've got a lot of he-said-she-said type of information but almost no physical evidence whatsoever. Not to mention, Fenway has some pull in this town. There are a lot of people trying to keep him out of trouble. I intend to pull this thread until his whole sweater unravels."

"What?" Baxter returned blankly.

"We want to know what you can tell us about your father and Dr. Schaffer, Baxter," Caine stated in a straightforward manner. "We know they were having an affair, and we know that Fenway was also romantically involved with Schaffer, but we have no evidence at the scene that either of those two were actually involved in the breakin outside a couple of less than credible informant."

"All I know about my father and Schaffer I learned from you guys. Well, and the letter in Schaffer's office, but she denied it existed."

"What do you remember about the letter and what did Schaffer say about it?"

"She said it wasn't from him or something. I know it was, but I never saw it again," Baxter spoke quickly, feeling a rush that he was speaking to Caine directly regarding the case. "I know you guys found other messages between them."

"That we did," smiled Caine, "Let me break down for you what we know and what we don't. We know that your therapist, Dr. Schaffer, was romantically involved with Fenway while she was having an affair with your father. We also believe your father was the target and your mother was collateral damage."

"Collateral damage?" Baxter asked.

"They didn't know your mother was there. She was killed because she was a witness," Caine explained.

"Jimmy..." Shabon whispered harshly. "This poor boy."

"I'm sorry, kid, I mean this is ancient history for you, right?" the detective asked.

"Yeah, I guess," Baxter offered, "I wish it felt more like that, but you're right." The young man shuffled his feet awkwardly, "I do still miss them."

"Of course you do, honey," Shabon smiled, touching his arm.

"Anyways," Caine pushed, "We believe your father was the target, and we think it was setup by someone in that little love triangle. Whether either of them actually did the deed, we don't know. They've both lawyered up, and neither are really cooperating much. It's a slippery case. We have bits of evidence pointing both ways and neither of them are helping to enlighten us. Frankly, I think they've both got dirty mitts."

"Are they going to court?" Baxter queried.

"That would be skipping some steps in the sequence. We need to build a decent case before we try. That's why I'm here. I've been running into dead ends, and you're the only one connected to everything. I need to know *everything* you know, even if it seems superfluous or unnecessary. Does that make sense?"

"It does, but I don't know anything. I didn't know my father and Schaffer were having an affair while I was in therapy. I never asked anything about it."

Caine tapped his pen against the notepad with a furrowed brow. "Well, shit," he muttered.

"You really believe it was one of them?" Baxter questioned.

"I'll tell you what, kid. I've been playing this game for a long time, and I'd bet dollars to donuts they were involved. Did they physically do it themselves? I doubt it. Fenway's a fucking weasel, but he's not a stupid one. Schaffer neither. If I was running the show, I'd plug 'em both in and let God figure it out. They both have information, that I'm absolutely certain of. They aren't coming clean; that's guilt to me. I just wish I knew why they aren't. It's almost like they're covering each other's tracks. That's not to say they're both necessarily guilty, but even if they're not, they're well aware that they're letting the murderer get away. My hands are tied, kid. There's not much I can do from here."

"Could they have done it together?" Baxter asked, developing an edge of frustration to his voice.

"Possibly. It would've been uncharacteristically sloppy

compared to everything else in the case. This was planned out by careful minds."

"They can't get away with it," the young man asserted.

"There can't be any doubt in the case," Shabon piped in. "They're going to walk out of the courtroom free as birds if we don't get hard evidence. Tell him what you have on Fenway, Jimmy."

"We have an informant that claims he overheard a vagrant chatting about being paid to do the job, but we don't have the vagrant, just the word of our informant, who's been a heroin addict for several years." Caine let out a deep sigh. "That won't play well in cross-examination. The obvious motive is jealousy."

"Do you believe your informant?" pressed the young man.

"Not because of who he is, but because of what he said. In his testimony to us, he described details of the murders that weren't published. Whoever he overheard knew things that only someone intimately acquainted with the crime could've known."

"Like?"

"He mentioned breaking *in* through the window, and that your mother.." Caine paused and exchanged concerned glances with Shabon.

"Baxter, do you feel comfortable talking about this stuff?" Shabon asked softly. "I know this is a difficult conversation for you."

"It's one that needs to be had," countered Caine with a murmur.

"No, I want to hear everything," Baxter stated intensely. "If this can end, I want it to as soon as possible."

Caine cleared his throat before continuing, "He knew your mother was the first person dispatched, and he knew your father was covered afterwards. Couldn't make that stuff up."

Baxter's jaw stiffened. His mother being killed first felt like a decent fifty-fifty guess, but the detail about his father being covered was definitely information from a source intimately acquainted with what transpired that night. "That's true," he stated intensely to Caine. "The comforter was over my father's head. He had to have been there to know that."

"That, or he's being given information from officers on the team," Caine replied.

"I can't believe any of our officers would give that kind of information away to someone outside the case," Shabon added.

Caine's face developed a wry smile, "Yeah right, I love our boys in blue, but a shot of whiskey and a round of Guinesses would milk that information out of them quicker than you could say chimichanga."

"I s'pose I just have more faith in our boys than you, detective," Shabon said defensively.

"And thank God you do, Officer Da'Brickashaw. They need all the faith they can get. It took me several years before I became sufficiently jaded, and I'm glad to hear you're still fighting the good fight for those boys."

"You think one of the officers at the scene may have told him the detail about my father?" Baxter asked anxiously.

"Honestly, no. Although, I've seen some real bone-headed moves by rookies at murder scenes, I agree with Shabon; I think it's the least likely explanation. No, I think the vagrant's story is an authentic account from someone intimately involved. And I think Schaffer and Fenway had something to do with it."

"I wish I knew something that could help," Baxter lamented. "I've told you everything I remember. Sometimes I wish I was older when it happened. If I'd been my age now, I feel like I could remember more important details."

"Don't worry about it, boss," Caine responded sympathetically. "I'm a bit of a bloodhound about these things. Once I catch a scent, I'm completely consumed, but this case's lack of evidence has caused me many sleepless nights."

"Do you think they're going to get away with it?" Baxter queried.

"Unless something changes and more comes up, I'm worried they will. I've been doing this for a while now, and that's part of the game. Some of these assholes just get away. Honestly, it requires a lot of mistakes for us to catch some of these guys."

"They can't get away with it," Baxter muttered resolutely.

"They *shouldn't* get away with it," Caine corrected. "There's one more planned interrogation with the two of them tomorrow at the station, but I don't imagine either of them are going to budge much or supply any new information. But you're a smart boy. I'm sure you've learned that the world doesn't care much for should."

"They can't get away with it," Baxter repeated to himself.

27

DIE MORITAT VON MACKLE MESSER

Shabon's radio buzzed twice before the police dispatcher's voice broke through the static with its unique brand of casual urgency.

"Officer six-three-seven, what's your twenty?" buzzed the radio.

Shabon reached up to her shoulder and tapped her speaker, "This is officer six-three-seven. I'm downtown at the intersection of Mercy and Madison. Over."

"We've got an assault at your location. Suspects gone rabbit. Paramedics en route. Rendezvous with Sgt. Peterson outside Sally's Diner."

"Affirmative, officer six-three-seven en route," Shabon barked as she hefted up her belt, spun around, and abruptly departed the apartment.

Baxter looked at Caine with wide eyes as his friend dashed out the door.

"Don't miss that," Caine chuckled. "I should probably head down there and see what's the rhubarb. You ok?"

"I'm fine," Baxter replied. "Is everything ok?"

"Not sure at the moment, but we'll make sure everything is safe. You're downtown, buddy. You pack this many people into a rundown block like this you're bound to have some of these shenanigans, but look at who I'm talking to. You know the type of animals that sulk around this neighborhood."

Baxter gently touched his wounded arm but made sure not to wince or give the appearance of too much discomfort. The injury served as his own reminder for just how rough the neighborhood was. He smirked as he looked out the window down at the streets that were slowly beginning to fill with inquisitive rubberneckers straining to find out what had happened outside the diner.

"You have any other information about Schaffer or that night that might help me before I go?" Caine asked as he adjusted his baseball cap and headed for the door.

"I'm sorry. I wish I had more, but there really wasn't anything for me to remember. I wasn't looking for clues..." the young man trailed off.

"Of course not. Look, I'll be in touch sometime after tomorrow's interview with Schaffer and Fenway. When do you work?"

"Evenings usually, after four."

"Roger," Caine winked and chuckled. "I'll drop by when I've got a sec."

"They can't get away with it," Baxter reminded the detective.

"I'm not planning on letting that happen, buddy," Caine returned with charismatic confidence.

When Shabon arrived at the scene outside Sally's, the Americana diner that Baxter had frequently admired but never actually entered, her first task was to clear the area of an ever growing crowd. Men and women from various walks of life littered the storefront that was being taped off by a couple of younger officers. As Shabon approached the roped off area, one of the officers dutifully lifted the tape and ushered her in. About halfway down the alleyway, there was a body covered by a dark shroud with a sizable pool of blood mixing with some restaurant litter.

"What's the story?" Shabon questioned the officer that had lifted the tape for her. "Dispatch called it out as assault, right?"

The younger officer chuckled grimly, "Eh, I'd say it may have started as assault half an hour ago. I think some folks inside the diner actually called it in, but by the time we got here the suspect had hightailed it outta here."

"The victim?" Shabon asked.

"Young kid," the officer sighed. "Put him at late teens, early twenties maybe. Doesn't look like he's wearing any gang apparel, but Hell if I know. I've seen those kids coming up with stupid, new gang accessories every fucking month."

"How far gone?"

"No pulse when we arrived. A couple liters of blood next to him. I'd imagine he bled out several minutes before we got here. Shit, looks like half a dozen stab wounds to his abdomen. Not wide, but deep punctures. Coulda been a switchblade. There was a doctor in the diner when we arrived; he made the call. Ambulance is a block over; one of the medics came by too and confirmed."

"Something needs to be done about these gangs out here. I had a tussle with a few of them yesterday evening. They were after some kid on the street and took off running when I put my lights on 'em," Shabon sneered as she craned her neck to peek down the alleyway again. A crime scene photographer wound his way around the officers and began snapping shots of the scene from various angles. "Oh well, guess I'll give a look." Shabon made her way down the alley amid the crank and pop of the camera's busy shutter. As she examined the pool of blood, it struck her how these scenes never seemed to become easier. The loss of life carried a profound aura. The idea that something as fundamental and basic as existence could also be so fragile made her feel uneasy as she approached the dark shroud. She knelt down beside the shroud and placed one hand against the alley wall for balance while she reached down and pulled the cover off the face of the body. "Oh dear," she muttered ruefully.

"You know this kid?" asked another officer.

"Not well, but I've seen him before," replied Shabon. "This stuff breaks my heart," she added, turning away.

"Monsters. If I find out which group of thugs did this..." she trailed off, her voice trembling.

One of the rookies reached his arm out and patted her back, "We'll find the fuckers. And when we do, we'll bury 'em."

Shabon smiled, but her eyes conveyed an authentic sadness. "Tired of this stuff happening," she sighed.

As the two officers commiserated, a high-pitched shriek permeated the gathered crowd and reverberated down the alleyway. Both officers jumped back in shock; the rookie reached down and unbuttoned his holster, but Shabon quickly calmed the green officer with a soft touch. Eventually, the crowd parted and a young girl with golden hair threw herself against one of the officers at the police tape.

"Max!" Eliza screamed hysterically as she pounded her clenched fists against the back of the officer who restrained her from continuing down the alley. "Max! Please no!" she sobbed in broken, trembling notes.

Shabon made eye contact with the officer at the tape and gestured for him to escort the young woman into the scene. "We're gonna need a positive identification anyways," she called to the front of the alley, "If this is who I think it is, she'll be able to verify."

When the officer lifted the tape to let Eliza into the alley, the girl dashed down the trash-filled street to the shrouded body. As she neared the corpse, she contemplated that which she was soon to behold. As her panic gave way to fear, her once swift feet turned to stone, and she finished the last few meters of her journey at a snail's pace.

Shabon recognized the trepidation in her gait and offered her a stabilizing hand. "What's your name again, Sweetie?"

"It-it's Eliza," she rasped, still trembling.

"Do you know who is under this sheet?" Shabon asked.

"I don't want it to be who I think it is."

Shabon gestured for the rookie officer to unveil the covered body. As the shroud was pulled from the face of the figure, Eliza let out a moan of anguish as she beheld the face of Max, his eyes open wide with horror.

Eliza fell to her hands and knees in the garbage and filth beside the body of Max. She clawed at the wet pavement and reached out to the face of her friend and confidant. Fresh tears fell from her face and dropped into the muddy puddles of the alley. The neon sign for Sally's Americana shone brilliantly in the dirty pools, producing a gaudy juxtaposition to the macabre and dingy crime scene in the alleyway. Shabon stood beside the young girl with her hand softly brushing back her long, golden hair, cooing comforting words to the devastated orphan.

"No, it can't be," Eliza sobbed. "Don't leave me, Max. This can't be happening."

Shabon wrapped her jacket around Eliza and pulled the girl up to her feet while motioning for the rookie to cover the body once more. She continued comforting the girl, "I'm sorry, baby. We're going to find out who did this. We're going to get those who were responsible."

"It doesn't matter," pined Eliza, wiping tears from her eyes. "Nothing matters."

20

BREAKIN' DOWN IS HARD TO DO

Shabon carefully escorted Eliza to a nearby ambulance, and as the paramedics checked the sobbing girls vitals, she gently probed concerning the circumstances of Max's presence in the area.

"Honey, we don't need to do this now, but the sooner we get some questions answered the better the chances that this doesn't happen to someone else," Shabon coaxed. "It's up to you to tell me that you're not ready, but I gotta couple questions for ya."

"Just ask," murmured Eliza with a despondent tone.

"What was Max doing down here?" she asked before whispering, *"Was he visiting Baxter?"*

"We visited Baxter early this morning, and we found him with drugs. Max got upset about it because Baxter is just making his life more difficult. He doesn't need help with that," the young girl responded still crying. "Baxter promised he'd stop using until we spoke to Sansarev. We told him Sansarev would know what to do."

"So you left Baxter's apartment? Then what?"

"We left his apartment and came out here to find somewhere to eat," Eliza whimpered.

"But Baxter didn't come?"

"No," she cleared her throat. "Max and I had been seeing each other for a few months, and we didn't want to tell Baxter yet. We thought he was too fragile for it. We just wanted to have a nice lunch together."

"Then what happened" Shabon pressed.

"We paid and left. When we passed this alley there was a guy in the alley that asked Max if he wanted to buy some drugs. Max was still angry about Baxter using again, and he yelled at the guy. He spat on the street in his direction. Not on the guy, but in his direction." At this point, Eliza had to stop speaking for a moment to regain her breath. Between her story and her sobs, she had run out of breath to continue either.

"There, there, honey. You take your time. There's no rush," Shabon reassured her.

"The guy lunged at Max, and the two of them tumbled back into the alley. They rolled around in the garbage for a while, and Max yelled at me to get the police. So I ran out into the street, yelling for help. I ran back into the diner to use the phone to call the police. I wanted to run back to him, but the dispatcher kept me on the phone to get more and more information. I should've just hung up when I heard sirens, but she told me to stay on the line."

"They always wanna keep you on the line to try and best assess the situation," Shabon remarked.

"I should've hung up when I heard the sirens so I could've been with him. Eventually, I told her the police had arrived, and I had to make sure he was OK. That was when I ran out and saw the crowd gathered by the tape. I saw the body, and I didn't want to believe it was Max-" she stopped and tried her best to hold in the sobs, but after a brief moment, the emotions were too much for the young girl to handle, and her body began to convulse as the sobs erupted once again. "How did it happen? Why is he dead?" she asked through broken gasps.

Shabon didn't answer immediately, but instead, continued to rub the young girl's shoulders. "He had several knife wounds to his abdomen," Shabon eventually replied. "One of the other officers think it may have been a switchblade. Easy to conceal."

"Max..." Eliza moaned.

"Can you tell me anything about the dealer?" Shabon asked softly.

"He had a hood over his head and wore dark sunglasses so I couldn't see his eyes. He was wearing a black sweatshirt and jeans. That's all I saw. No, wait. When they first started fighting, his hood came halfway off. He had blonde hair. Dirty blond."

"Age?"

"Our age, I guess. Maybe early twenties."

"Race?"

"White."

"That's good honey. That's real good," Shabon praised the girl as she reached up to her radio, "I need an APB put out on a Caucasian male, early twenties, possibly wearing jeans and a black, hooded sweatshirt in relation to the stabbing outside Sally's Diner on Madison."

"What do I do?" asked Eliza as she wiped tears away and stood up.

"You've done everything you can, sweetie," responded Shabon. "I think we need to get you to a safe and restful place. How would you feel about me calling Mr. Sansarev and having him pick you up?"

"I think that would be good," Eliza answered before a renewed wave of tears began flooding her eyes, "Will you tell him what happened? I can't do it. I don't want to hurt him."

29

THE IRREPARABLE II

Once Caine left the apartment, Baxter perched himself beside the window ledge and looked out over the gathering crowd. His apartment didn't face the proper direction to grant him a clear view of the event, but he was able to witness the growing crowd that grew with every passing minute around Sally's. He desperately wished to leave Stonegate for a better vantage point of the situation, but with all the police converging on the area, he knew he'd instantly be recognized and arrested. He sat at the window sill for hours, pressed against the glass for the optimal viewpoint. Eventually, he retired from his perch and lay down on his mattress due to his inability to witness anything except the murmuring spectators.

He continued to perseverate on his conversation with Shabon and Caine and was furious that neither Fenway nor Schaffer were cooperating with police. He took a deep breath to calm down and closed his eyes as he heard ambulance sirens whur away from the block. He'd grown accustomed to the loud emergency sirens blaring around downtown Morristown, and after his conversation with Caine and Shabon, he didn't feel compelled to investigate the misfortunes of others. He listened as the crowd dispersed and the sound of muttering dissipated into the early evening air. Those lucky observers who'd seen their dose of senseless violence for the day continued on their way, numb to the value of their own health. Baxter exhaled deeply and his eyes grew heavy as he began formulating a plan.

Immediately upon hearing of the tragedy that took place downtown, Sansarev had Karel pick up Eliza and escort her back to St. Joseph's posthaste. As the young woman entered the orphanage, her old housemaster stood in the atrium with wet eyes and outstretched arms. "Angel!" he cried.

"Sansarev!" the girl sobbed with a renewed wave of anguish. She fell into the Russian's arms, and the two emotionally embraced each other, both doing their best to hold back their gasping breaths.

"You're safe, child," the housemaster reassured soothingly. "There's nothing here to worry you. You're always safe here, and we'll always take care of you."

Eliza clutched Sansarev's jacket and continued to cry, "Everything is so terrible. So terrible, so terrible..." she trailed off in a catatonic state. Sansarev just held her gently and pressed his grey beard down on her head.

"I know, child. We're living in dark days. I've always tried to protect you from them, but it seems there was little I could do. This world can be a very scary place."

Alejandra came scuttling out of the dining room with her mascara running down the sides of her face, "Eliza, my sweet flower; I heard. I'm so sorry."

Sansarev grimaced as Eliza shook more violently within his grasp. Every well-intentioned apology or show of empathy further reminded her as to the fountainhead of her sorrow. "Max, please come back..."

Alejandra bit her bottom lip to hold in her own cries and wrapped her arms around Eliza and Sansarev. A couple of young children came into the living room and were taken aback to see the three huddled together in a mass of soulful sobs, but the adults didn't notice, and shortly after the children had entered, the young ones turned around with looks of fearful concern and hurriedly departed the melancholy scene.

"You'll be staying here until you feel well enough to venture back out," Sansarev eventually stated absolutely. "We're family, and we need each other now."

"I'll run you a bath, angel, and get you some hot tea," Alejandra offered as she covered her face with a hand.

Sansarev looked up suddenly like a deer caught in the headlights and asked, "Does Baxter know? Did you speak to him?"

Eliza rubbed her eyes and whimpered, "No he doesn't.

We saw him earlier that morning at his place, but everything happened once we left. He doesn't know anything."

Sansarev stood still for just a moment before grabbing a coat from the foyer and heading to the doorway. "Alejandra will take care of you tonight. I'll be back shortly to make sure everything is OK. I just want to make sure Baxter doesn't do anything rash when he hears about what happened. He's not in a mindset to handle news like this."

It was well after midnight before Karel pulled up to the Stonegate apartments, and Sansarev swiftly slipped out of his automobile. Karel knocked on his dash three times as Sansarev departed and wished his friend good luck. Sansarev charged up the stairs to Baxter's apartment, dashed down the long corridor, and forcefully knocked on the door to awaken the boy. He wasn't sure if Baxter had learned the news from anyone else yet, but he knew the young man would be in a dire place if he didn't have the appropriate support present during the Hellish discovery. As Sansarev stood impatiently at the door, waiting for any kind of answer to come from the apartment, his mind reminisced on memories of Max and Baxter as young boys, taking part in one another's hi-jinx several years earlier when they were new arrivals to St. Joseph's. Sansarev rapped against the door again, but there was still no answer. "Mr. Bishop, it's me. Sansarev. I need to speak with you," he commanded in an authoritative voice. "Baxter, please open the door. I need to speak to you now." There was still no answer. The housemaster slammed his fist hard against the door and cried, "Baxter!"

Still, the solid door remained closed, and no signs of life came from the young man's apartment. Sansarev took two steps back and charged at the door with his shoulder down, striking the portal with his weight. The door shook and the hinges buckled under the force, but the door remained standing. Sansarev moaned and held his shoulder that had been badly injured in the attempt, but he knew he couldn't relent. The old housemaster turned his body, dropped his other shoulder down, and charged the door with determination once again. A loud pop came from the door, the hinges exploded off the frame, and the housemaster fell face-first into the apartment. Every window was open, and every light had been left on, but the troubled orphan was nowhere to be found. Sansarev looked out the window toward the ground below but was relieved to find the sidewalks beneath the window empty.

He spun around in a circle quickly scanning the room for any sign of the where the young man could've head, but there were no clues visible to him. The apartment remained much as it was the last time he'd visited. Finally the housemaster pressed his back against the wall and clutched his right arm. His voice trembled as he exhaled and mumbled to himself, "Baxter, son, wherever you are; be smart."

30

DRAWN TO THE DAWN

"I know you can help me, Stretch," Baxter urged his friend. "You might not have anything, but I know you know people that do."

"Listen, man, I don't mess with that stuff. That shit brings nothin' but trouble. Everyone that plays the gun game runs into some motherfucker that's got a bigger gun," Stretch explained with a smoking gun gesture. "Trust me, man. Only a real dumbass with a deathwish puts that much money in the pot."

"I don't need to explain myself to you, Stretch, and I know you can get me something. Just hook me up. Don't make me do this the hard way."

"Hard way?" asked Stretch incredulously, "Whaddya know about the hard way?"

"Look, I like you, but I need a gun. If I have to, I'll walk right out of here and tell a cop everything going on in this little apartment closet," Baxter persuasively threatened.

"Makin' threats and shittin' on my home, eh?" Stretch spat, "Yeah, you're a real good friend."

"I'm sorry, Stretch," the orphan apologized, "Give me what I need, and you don't have to worry about anything else."

"I've had a lot of crackheads come in here sayin' that exact same shit." Stretch paused for a moment, looking thoughtfully towards Baxter. Stretch wrinkled his nose in thought, "But something tells me you've got bigger plans than most of the street fucks that demand shit around here." Stretch crossed the tiny apartment and reached under his couch. He felt around for several seconds before he pulled out a large book of nursery rhymes. He noticed Baxter's raised eyebrows at the tome, and he smiled broadly, "The only thing I have left from my ma. I *think* she used to read these to me when I was a baby."

"You kept it all these years?" Bater replied. "Good for you. Every day I wish I could've held onto my childhood more."

"Yeah right," Stretch dismissed with a morbid snicker as he opened the book's covers to reveal hollowed out pages containing a black revolver with a handsome, wooden grip, and a sprinkling of bullets. "Trust me, the gun's a better symbol of my childhood." Stretch picked the handgun up and gingerly tossed it back and forth in his hands like a toy before spinning it around and handing it to Baxter.

The orphan took the gun with great respect and held the instrument with awe, admiring its potential for profound change. He grabbed a handful of bullets from the book and meticulously loaded them into the six cylinders. "Feels weird holding it," Baxter commented.

"I agree," Stretch echoed. "Always scared me to death just thinkin' bout using it. Six bullets? Sounds like you're going to be busy."

Baxter chuckled, "Actually, I've just never used one before. I'm not planning on missing, but I don't want to take any chances."

"What are you planning on doing?" Stretch asked.

"It's better you don't know," Baxter replied as he concealed the revolver in his jacket. "Stretch?"

"Yeah?"

"I'm sorry about this, but I should let you know. You won't see me again."

"You're taking my gun, and I won't see you again?" Stretch repeated, his mouth agape.

"That's right," Baxter smiled. "Thanks for your help, man."

"Don't do anything stupid," Stretch advised as the orphan opened the door and the cold night wind swept into the apartment.

"Stretch?"

"Yeah?"

"I'm sorry about what I said about your place. Honestly, I really like it here."

"Thanks, you ol' dumpster diver," Stretch replied as the orphan disappeared into the blackness.

Baxter had no issues finding the police station as the sun rose, and the morning streets were flooded with citizens seeing to their normal lives. He concealed himself in a small cluster of bushes about fifty meters from the entrance and waited patiently. Although he hadn't slept the previous night, he remained alert at his post, restlessly observing the station's front parking lot. After a little over an hour, Baxter grit his teeth as he observed Dr. Veronica Schaffer entering through the station's main entrance. He recognized Detective Caine greeting her inside the station's all glass doors. The two stood their for a few moments, idly chatting before another man walked into the station, flanked on both sides by well dressed professionals. *"Fenway?"* Baxter whispered under his breath. As the man opened the station door, Baxter saw his smile; a smile that spoke of confidence in his defense but fear in his soul. The group remained in the lobby for only a few minutes exchanging pleasantries before they disappeared in the station lobby. Baxter remained still in the bushes until he was certain no one would detect him. Once all was clear, he swiftly dashed into the parking lot and ran to Fenway's vehicle. The car's doors were locked; however, there were small gaps in both the backdoors' windows. Baxter quickly spun his head around to determine whether anyone was watching him before he jumped up and pushed down on the windows with all his strength. With each push, the car windows would grudgingly creak down a fraction of an inch, until finally, Baxter was able to squeeze his hand inside the vehicle and manually unlock the car. The back of the car had a few coats that the young man used to hide as he wedged himself behind the driver's seat. His new spot was uncomfortable, and after an hour, he felt his legs going numb. He'd occasionally straighten them but decided to remain in his position as long as possible to lessen any chance he'd be caught. Time passed slowly, but Baxter was contently fixated on his objective.

After another hour passed, Baxter heard voices growing louder as they entered the parking lot. Caine was speaking to Schaffer and a couple of unknown characters. They were still too far from the car for Baxter to discern anything they said. Inside the vehicle and underneath the blankets, every word sounded like a muddled blur, but eventually, the voices became clearer as they drew closer to the car. He closed his eyes and prayed that he'd remain undetected. Not before long, some of the voices became clearer as they closed in on the vehicle.

"Great work in there, gentlemen. You know I appreciate you guys doing this for me. I don't imagine we'll be spending too much more time in that station," one man said.

"At this point, they're just wasting everyone's time," commented another. "The last two times we've gone in there it's been for essentially nothing. No new evidentiary developments, just fresh accusations."

"Next time they bring us in without anything, I'm

going to speak to some people and see if there's nothing we can do to squash this thing for good," said the third.

"Nothing would make me happier," replied the first voice. "I have my own practice to run," he laughed.

"Just keep out of their crosshairs, Pat. You'll be fine," the third chuckled.

"This is an old game for me, Mike. Thanks again for all your help. I'm going to get out of here. Makes me nauseated to be here off the clock and without a client. Even worse than pro bono shit," he guffawed as he opened his car door and slid into the driver's seat. "I'm certain this thing is dead, but if they try and weasel out any more developments, keep me in the loop."

"You got it, Pat. Be safe."

The voices continued, but they became quieter as the gentlemen headed to their own vehicles. Fenway turned the ignition and pulled out of the station's lot. He laughed as he tapped on his steering wheel along to the radio, whistling with contentment.

Baxter stayed deathly silent as he watched trees fly by through the far window. The view reminded him of his first ride in a police car, heading downtown after his parents' death. He remembered watching the bustling, happy world and felt the anxious teeth sink into his heart that his life would be forever different, forever colder. For him, the passage of time had stopped, and his world had frozen into a hideous existence. He'd spent the better part of the last decade searching for a way to thaw his icy empire, but his best laid plans had brought him to his current circumstance, hiding in the backseat of a stranger's car beneath a pile of coats. His sweaty palm gripped the revolver tightly in his hand; his fingers gently rubbing against the cold, metal cylinder. *"How dare I consider him a stranger,"* Baxter thought. *"As if he had no real impact on my life. I wish he was truly a stranger. I wish I didn't know him, who he was, and what he'd done."*

"Do you *know* what he's done?" asked Cassius, casually sitting in the passenger seat. "Let's save the sentence for *after* the verdict, aye, young'un?"

"I know enough," Baxter thought, *"And I'm not pulling the trigger. He's going to tell me more before today's done."*

"Jus' don't get ahead of yourself, kid. You're holdin' a trial of sorts right now, and ugly stuff comes out at trials. Stuff you didn't want to know."

"I can't escape it all until I know it all."

Baxter estimated they must be at least a few miles from the station now, and although his plan was becoming more impromptu with each passing second, he decided now was the time to act. He adjusted his sweaty hands on the revolver's grip, rose from the backseat, pulled back the hammer, and placed the barrel against the man's neck.

"I'm *not* going to kill you now," Baxter tried to say with a clear monotone voice, but the adrenaline coursing through his body caused the pitch of his voice to tremble and oscillate awkwardly.

"Fuck!" Fenway screamed as the car veered a few feet from its lane.

"Drive straight!" Baxter ordered sternly, pressing the barrel harder into the driver's neck.

Fenway heeded the orphan's command and did his best to maintain normal driving habits. "Look kid, I don't have much money on me. Everything I have is your's, including this car if you want it. I won't even report it stolen. Everything I've got, your's. You just have to let me live," Fenway whimpered, attempting to conceal his fear but failing greatly.

"You've already taken everything from me," Baxter calmly replied. "I don't want what you have; I want *back* what you *took*."

"Who are you!? I've never taken anything from you!" he shouted, "I don't even know who the Hell you are!"

"You took my parents from me," Baxter stated coldly.

"Oh Christ!" Fenway spat, "What did those fucking cops tell you? Listen kid, you can't listen to them. They're making stuff up. It's all complete lies!"

Baxter exhibited a wry smile. He was enjoying the immense power he felt having absolute dominion over his enemy. "Don't worry, Patrick. You're going to tell me everything, but let me tell you how this is going to work."

"Anything you want," Fenway pleaded.

"Take me to Schaffer."

"Veronica? I don't know where she is."

"Call her."

"Of course," Fenway agreed as he picked up his phone and rang Schaffer. "Hey Veronica. Yeah, it's Pat. I need to meet you-"

"In private," Baxter interrupted with a whisper.

"I need to meet you in private, immediately," continued

Fenway. "I can't talk now. Meet me at my place? Okay, okay, where would you like? OK, got it, your place. I'm on my way now."

"Ready the stage lights!" laughed Cassius jubilantly, "This is about to get intense."

"I'm taking us to her place," Fenway explained. "You want me to tell you the truth?"

"Not yet," Baxter replied. "Take us to Schaffer's. Anything goes wrong; you die."

Fenway pressed further down on the accelerator and took a left. For the first several blocks, he remained quiet, but eventually the extreme anxiety of the situation got the better of him, and he began trembling. "Look, kid," he pleaded. "This whole thing got out of hand, but I promise you, I had nothing to do with your parents. I didn't even know your parents. I'm sure they were great folks."

Baxter remained silent as the car sped on.

"I barely knew my parents," Fenway blurted out while his eyes darted frantically around the streets for a way out of his current predicament. "It's tough not having parents around. I get that, but I didn't have anything to do with your parents death. That's a fact and a promise."

"Shut up," Baxter replied gravely. "Just drive."

31

REVELATIONS

*"No man, for any considerable period,
can wear one face to himself and another
to the multitude, without finally getting
bewildered as to which may be the true."*
- Nathaniel Hawthorne -

B axter felt his heart race as Fenway pulled up Schaffer's driveway. The orphan kept his head down to preserve the element of surprise. He knew his old therapist had the potential to be extremely persuasive, and unlike Fenway, she had at least some idea of what Baxter knew and what he didn't. Fenway's lies would have been easy to sift through. Schaffer's had the possibility of being much more convincing. Baxter foresaw his salvation coming from the two of them together. If they were protecting each other from Caine, Baxter intended to see how forthcoming they'd be when the pursuit of justice wasn't being equivocated by the camouflage of the court-room. In Baxter's court there would be no oaths. If you were willing to lie, it was naive to believe an oath would stop you from doing so. But a gun? The tangibility of the bullet was its greatest deterrent. The revolver offered no ambiguities, no vague suggestions. The cold, metal hand-cannon was absolute in its retribution; the wielder's truth never escaped.

"Walk in slowly," Baxter ordered. "You run; I shoot. You only speak when I tell you to. I ask the questions; you give the answers. Understood?"

Fenway nodded and exhaled, "Should I head in now?"

"Yes."

Fenway stepped out of the car and entered the home; Baxter followed closely behind with the gun covered by one of the coats he'd taken from the back seat. Schaffer was seated on a couch in the living room when the two men arrived. "What's with all the mystery, Patrick? Why did you get off the phone-" she froze when Baxter came through the doorway. "Baxter?!"

"Hello Dr. Shaffer," the young man spoke with an icy calm as he pulled the revolver from underneath the coat. He kept its barrel trained on Fenway. "I'm here for the truth. I know the two of you are protecting each other, and I brought the gun to end that. There are truths I know, and there are some I don't. I admit that. What's going to happen here is I'm going to ask the two of you questions, and you will answer me. If I know you're lying, I may warn you, or I may shoot you. It depends on the lie. You may not speak to each other, only me. Fenway, have a seat on the couch."

Fenway obeyed and quietly sat on the couch a few feet from Schaffer. He gave Schaffer a deeply concerned glance, but the doctor didn't acknowledge him.

"Baxter, please be careful with that weapon," Schaffer warned, trying to remain calm. "You're making a big mistake."

"I know I might be, but I don't see myself as having much to lose. The last few days I've thought about how much easier it would be just to end everything. There's nothing I really want from this world anymore, except this. I need to know the truth, and I have to do something reckless to get it. Well-," he brandished the gun, "Here it is."

"You're not a murderer, Baxter," Schaffer reasoned. "You're young. You have so much more to live for...so much more time."

"You see time, and you see possibility. I see time, and I see suffering. That's how different our perspectives are. Understand that none of your hopefulness makes sense to me. It hasn't for a long time. But now, I've decided to take that hopelessness, that emotion that's dragged me through the gutter for many years and use it to my advantage. My life means nothing to me, and your life means nothing to me. His life means nothing to me," he said, pointing the gun at Fenway. When I ask you questions, remember that," Baxter took a deep breath and grinned. "Before a single word comes out of your mouth that may not be true, remember that pulling this trigger means nothing to me."

"Baxter-" Schaffer began pleading before being cut off.

"Question one is for you, doctor," the orphan said as he turned the gun back to her. "Were you sleeping with my father before he died?"

"Baxter, this is ridic-" she began before the revolver interrupted her with a thunderous boom. The bullet struck the throw pillow leaning against her left thigh and exploded into a deluge of downy feathers. Schaffer screamed and clutched herself in terror.

"The truth, and nothing but the truth, so help you God," the orphan reminded her. "Did you have a relationship with my father before he died?"

Schaffer closed her eyes as she began crying and muttered the word, "Yes."

"You told me the letter I found wasn't from him."

"I lied," she rasped as she began sobbing. "Please don't kill me."

Baxter sighed, "I told you. That's not how the game works. The truth shall set you free. Fenway?"

"Yes," Fenway replied as the gun barrel slowly swooped over to him.

"Were you sleeping with Veronica and did you know she was sleeping with my father?"

Fenway attempted another glance at Schaffer for aid, but he received none. "I-um-yes. Baxter, if I can just explain-"

Baxter recocked the revolver's hammer and silenced Fenway.

"Veronica," the orphan continued, foregoing etiquette, "Did you have anything to do with my parents' death?"

The doctor took a deep breath and tried to hold back her tears as she spoke, "I'd like to believe I didn't, Baxter. I honestly hope I didn't, but we were in a relationship. There were stresses in our lives because of that. Stresses that could've caused whatever happened to happen."

Baxter hesitated briefly at Schaffer's ambiguous comment. "Fenway," Baxter continued. "Did you have anything to do with my parents' death?"

Fenway shifted on the couch, and his leg started to shake involuntarily, "Don't listen to her, Baxter! She set the entire thing up!"

"Patrick, you lying piece of shit!" Schaffer yelled.

"Quiet!" Baxter boomed. "Tell me what she's making up, and you better convince me it's the truth."

"She told me she had to kill him, but she couldn't go through with it herself! She hired someone else to do her dirty work. She wanted out of the relationship with your father, but your dad refused. He first saw her as a patient and threatened to come clean about the affair if she ended it. She said it would've ended her career. Decades of her life, gone! That's why she wanted him dead. She asked me if I could handle it, and I said I'd never be involved in something like that. I'm a lawyer, son. I know how these things end up. It's my livelihood-"

"You're a fucking snake, Patrick!" Schaffer shouted furiously.

Baxter turned the iron sight to Schaffer, "Explain."

Schaffer started sobbing louder, and she wiped the tears from her eyes as she began, "I did meet your father as a client first. He wasn't happy in his marriage. It was stupid of me to take him on as a patient. I was attracted to him immediately. Your father and I ended up becoming romantically involved. It's true," she gasped for breath between her sobs, "But we loved each other. I stopped feeling that way for Patrick. When I told Patrick that I had developed feelings for someone else, he became irate. He found out who it was and threatened to kill him if I ended our relationship-"

"Oh Jesus," Fenway sneered, "Spare us the soap opera, Veronica. Your lies have become exhausting."

"Don't you realize it's all over, you idiot," Schaffer fired back. "He hired some bum from downtown to do it, to kill your father. Your mother wasn't even-" Schaffer broke down into more violent weeping. "Your mother never did anything to deserve what happened."

"But you gave her the worst of it didn't you!?" charged Fenway.

"I'm so sorry, Baxter," Schaffer cried. "For years, I've wanted nothing more than to rewind time and never meet your father. It was why I searched for you at the orphanage. My dream-governance therapy was real, as you know, but I wanted to help you because I recognized my role in hurting you."

"If you knew this was going on, why didn't you go to the police?" Fenway snarled. "Your story falls apart so easily. Can we *please* take this to court?"

"If your story is true," Baxter interjected, "Why were you withholding information?"

"Oh ho! A great question!" chuckled Fenway. "Let's see how you handle this young man's cross-examination."

"I threatened to years ago, Baxter," Schaffer replied. "Eventually the remorse was too much. Even when I was helping you, I felt consumed with resent. My career meant nothing to me after the incident between you and Eliza. I saw Brent allowing me to work with you as a second chance, but I never forgave myself. I wanted to tell the police everything, but Patrick told me he'd planted evidence that would incriminate me. If I went to the police with what I knew, he'd go to the police with what he'd planted. It wasn't my career he'd take. It'd be my life."

"What evidence?" Baxter pushed.

"He wouldn't tell me. I never knew what it was. Just that he said it existed."

"Baxter, what you're going to find with Veronica is a web of pathways that all lead to dead ends. Various scenarios, that can't be proven mind you, where she remains blameless, and not just blameless, but the victim!" Fenway rubbed his temples in frustration. "I've told you what happened. My story doesn't require any extra questions or new discoveries. She needed your father out of the picture to save her career, and she did what she believed was necessary."

"What evidence do you have on her?" Baxter queried.

"Evidence that she did it? I know she did it," he

laughed. "The only reason I know all of this was because she told me. There's no planted evidence. I've never had anything to do with your parents. Ever."

"If there's no evidence on me, I'll go to the police right now and tell them everything. My entire story. I'm certain they'll be able to put it together with what they know," Schaffer offered.

Baxter noticed Fenway hesitate briefly before responding, "By all means, Baxter. Take us back to the station with threat of violence! Keep that barrel pointed at the back of our heads the entire way. We'll walk right in there with our attorneys, and she can provide all the testimony against me that she wishes. She can slander and libel my good name with every lie she can come up with. It won't stick because it's not the truth. That's the beauty of the justice system. We don't wallow around in emotions and conjecture. We require evidence to ensure we don't make mistakes in judgement."

"This guy's a songbird," Cassius quipped from the back of the room. "I have to say, kid, in some ways you're lucky."

"How's that?" Baxter asked.

"Honestly, between the two of these Sobbing Sallies, I don't think you've got a bullet to waste." Cassius chuckled as he pantomimed wiping crying eyes.

"Evidence assures us that we don't carry out vigilante justice based on our emotions, like you're doing now. Evidence lets us know that we're pursuing the truth, not the latest fairy tale told by a pretty psychologist that I have no doubt has done her best to seduce your young mind," Fenway declared.

"He's right that she's not bad to look at," smiled Cassius, tilting his head over the couch to admire Schaffer.

"Let the courts handle this, son," Fenway continued. "It's the only way to spare your conscience from the horrible aftermath of a wrong judgement. Trust me, as a lawyer, I've been there. You don't want to add that to your list of regrets."

Baxter contemplated Fenway's suggestion, and he hated the sense it made.

"Baxter," Schaffer offered between whimpers, "I hesitate to say this because I'm terrified of you right now, but if you let him go, and he did plant evidence, he's going to be just as immune in that police station as he was before this happened. He loses nothing from telling you the planted evidence doesn't exist. You have no way of knowing, but if it does, he has the ability to turn this entire thing away from him whenever he wants."

"Think about this, son. She literally doesn't want the *evidence* to come out. Can you imagine hearing anything so guilt-ridden. In my three decades of practicing law, I've *never* had an innocent client tell me they didn't want evidence coming out. It just doesn't happen."

"It's not real evidence, Baxter," Schaffer asserted, "And his bullshit is an insult to your intelligence."

"Quiet! Both of you!" Baxter roared. His head was spinning. He'd imagined this confrontation being much more enlightening; instead, he stood in a room with a law-yer and a psychologist that deftly twisted his thoughts in various ways. Nothing seemed trustworthy. His emotions, his instincts, his reasoning, his intellect...everything was being manipulated.

32

CASSIUS' HOOK

"**D**id you ever love her?" Baxter asked Fenway, pointing to Schaffer.

"I had strong feelings for her at one point," Fenway confessed, "But I don't know if I'd call it love. Consider it lust," he grinned. "I don't know if she was ever as amicable to you as she was towards your father, but I can promise you, she's a wildcat of a lay. Those smooth, firm legs wrapped around you?" Fenway whistled.

"You disgusting, despicable monster," Schaffer snarled. "I wish I had the gun. I'd kill you myself."

"Well if you needed more proof that she's got the will to kill!" Fenway slapped his leg as he laughed. "I'm glad our relationship was more of a bedroom transaction. You'd be impossible to defend in a courtroom, Veronica. You don't threaten to kill people when you're being tried for murder."

Baxter noticed Cassius adopt a pensive countenance

as he stared out the window. Eventually the older man turned to Baxter and grinned from ear to ear. "I have an idea, young'un," and he nodded his head towards another room in the house.

"If either of you leave this room, you die," Baxter warned with a fiery glare as he departed the living room.

"Justice is on my side, son; I have nothing to fear," Fenway replied with a broad smile.

After a few minutes, Baxter returned to the living room where Schaffer and Fenway had resorted to a vicious argument.

"You're a foul piece of garbage," Schaffer snarled.

"I think we've already established you can't be trusted. How many more lies do you think your pretty little lips will get away with before you lose all credibility. Shouldn't a therapist understand the importance of trust and rapport?" Fenway retorted.

"Enough, you two!" Baxter shouted. "You're both the most deceitful people I've ever met. If you'd just told the truth to Detective Caine, you wouldn't even be here, but here we are. I don't trust either of you. Neither of you trust each other. As far as I see it you're both guilty. If not of the actual murder then guilty of this bullshit cover for each other."

"Baxter, I swear to you, if you let me go I will tell Caine *everything* I know. I don't care what traps this bastard has planted, but I don't care. I'll tell Caine everything," Schaffer pleaded.

"She's a dirty liar, but I think it's your best bet," Fenway agreed. "You can't kill us in cold blood. That isn't the kind of resolution you want. You'll be hunted down immediately."

Cassius sneered at them both, "These two sure do talk a lot when their own hides are on the line."

Baxter nodded at his friend. "You're both right, sadly. I don't know which of you was responsible for my parents' death. I do know you're both liars, and I've decided to let the two of you choose how this ends." With a smile, Baxter tossed the revolver between the two, slightly closer to Schaffer.

Both Schaffer and Fenway's reactions were instantaneous. Schaffer lunged for the handgun on the ground, but just as she slipped her fingers around the handle, Fenway's shoulder drove hard into her torso sending her flying against the wall. She was able to keep her hand on the gun but was unable to recover from the blow before Fenway was on top of her with one hand clutching her outstretched wrist.

"You'd love to gun me down and pawn this all off on me, wouldn't you, Veronica?" Fenway growled as the two grappled on the ground. Schaffer clawed at his face and bit down on his clavicle. Fenway roared in pain, reared up, and headbutted Schaffer in the right temple. The blow was incapacitating, and Schaffer's strikes become weaker and weaker until her hands flailed defenselessly against his body.

"You'll pay for your sins, Veronica," Fenway hissed as he

repeatedly bashed her hand against the wall. Eventually, her grip loosened, and the gun fell from her fingertips. Fenway picked up the revolver and held it against her head as her blue eyes looked up with a wounded vacancy. "You know what, Veronica?" he spat as he reached his hand down, separating her legs and pushing himself between her thighs, "Maybe I'll fuck you one last time to make up for the thorn in my side you're so intent on being. How would that feel?" he asked as he reached down to unbuckle his belt.

"Bax-" Schaffer mouthed breathlessly.

"Ah, you're right!" Fenway barked. "The idiot boy. Before I take my pound of flesh from you, I need to do what I should've done a long time ago. Didn't know there was a kid, but time to deal with this loose end."

Fenway pointed the revolver at Baxter as he laughed sinisterly, "You're a fool, kid. And now you're a dead fool. For the record, I didn't personally kill your parents, but I did pay a psychopathic lowlife to. He told me your mother was a particularly messy death. He took his time with her." Fenway slapped Schaffer's face a couple of times to keep her conscious. "This little situation you've put me in is going to make my court case much more difficult, but I don't mind. The satisfaction I'm going to get hollowing out your skull combined with one last evening with Dr. Schaffer here," he giggled maniacally as he caressed her neck down to her chest. "I may just make myself at home for a couple days. Use you as I see fit, Veronica."

Fenway pulled back on the revolver hammer, pointed it at Baxter, and pulled the trigger.

33

JUSTICE BLENDER

The gun clicked as the hammer fell on an empty cylinder. Fenway cursed and fanned the hammer several times before realizing the bullets had been removed from the weapon. "You clever little fuck," Fenway growled. "But not too clever. I'm going to beat the hell out of you, just like her." He wrapped a hand around Schaffer's neck, squeezing slightly and whispering, "I'll be back for you, babe." He stood up, smiling at the young man, "Time to see what kind of man you are, boy."

"I'd never felt in control of a situation more than I did pointing that gun at you two," Baxter conceded. "I knew you'd feel the same way." The orphan chuckled, "I've never enjoyed seeing people in pain, but I have the feeling I'm going to find a lot of pleasure in this." The young man pulled two large kitchen knives from behind his back. "Don't get your hopes up, asshole. They're both for me."

Fenway threw the revolver at Baxter's head, but the gun flew harmlessly over his left shoulder. "You little prick," Fenway sighed. "You do this, you're going to prison. You know that, right? Ya know what happens to little boys like you in prison? They're going to love you."

"I may. I've been there before," Baxter replied calmly. "Going to prison will be a small price to pay to send you to Hell."

The young man brandished the kitchen knives and leapt at Fenway. He swung the first blade wildly, and Fenway dodged easily, but the second found its mark as it tore across Fenway's abdomen, leaving a deep bloody gash in the man's midsection.

"We can make a deal, kid," Fenway offered as he held his hand against the grievous wound. "I can give you more money than you can imagine. I can completely turn around your life. You're just a destitute orphan. You kill me and that's still all you're going to be. Spare me, and I'll make you a millionaire."

"Your dealmaking days are over, you bastard," Baxter replied as he simultaneously slashed at Fenway's face with one blade while stabbing at his gut with the other. Fenway threw his head back to avoid the slashing blade but gasped as the other knife dug into his stomach. Blood oozed from the open wounds as Fenway stumbled back into the wall, clutching his abdomen.

"Have fun in prison, you-" Fenway gasped as Baxter ran one of the knives under his chin and up through the bottom of his jaw. The knife handle stuck out from the floor of his mandible as Fenway gurgled unintelligibly before collapsing on the ground.

Baxter watched the blood run down the man's neck and stain his shirt red. The boy looked over to Schaffer who was still on the verge of losing consciousness. He knelt beside his old therapist and held her head in his hands as her eyes fluttered languidly. "I can't stay here, Schaffer. I have to disappear. You can tell them whatever you want about what happened; it doesn't matter to me. I wish I knew where the mask ended and you began, but for what it's worth, I appreciate the help you've given me. I wish it hadn't come to this. Terror has made me cruel."

34

A FAREWELL TO HARMS

Detective Caine and Shabon pulled up to St. Joseph's orphanage for what they both wished would be the last time. Baxter had disappeared into the wind after the altercation at Schaffer's home. Besides a fairly severe concussion, the psychologist had survived with minimal wounds and relayed the entirety of the episode to investigators as soon as the police arrived. When the two law enforcement officers entered the building, Eliza and Alejandra greeted them and led them up the stairs to Sansarev's study.

"So, sounds like our boy took matters into his own hands," Caine said as he vigorously shook Sansarev's hand. "Wish it didn't have to go down like that, but I guess he wasn't interested in waiting."

"Nothing had been solved in a while," Alejandra countered. "Seems like he was the only person to actually get anything done."

"I've never claimed the justice system works quickly," Caine laughed. "I wager I could count my open cases on one hand if I could interview suspects with a gun to their head."

"Din't Flannery O'Connor write a story bout that?" asked Shabon.

"About what?" Caine replied.

"Bout how people behave better when there's a gun to their head."

"They do," Caine chuckled, "They most certainly do. What about you, Sergei? How're you feeling about your boy's final day among us."

"It breaks my heart," answered Sansarev with a deep sigh. "The pain of that boy's existence. Walking around with that weight. I wouldn't wish it on any man, but for a child...?"

"I saw glimpses of such goodness in that boy," Alejandra added. "I'll always remember Mr. Bishop running through the gardens with Seth and Max, chasing girls and causing good-natured mischief." Eliza buried her face in her hands, and Alejandra wrapped her arms around the girl. "I'm sorry, baby. I forgot you were here."

"Makes me wonder," Caine spoke wistfully. "What could that boy's life have been? Who was he supposed to be before all this mess came down like an avalanche?"

Sansarev looked out the window of his study as he played with one of the baubles from his desk. He spoke slowly as he surveyed the children playing in the gardens below, "How innocent are we?" He paused for a long

239

moment, contemplating questions he'd been asking himself for years. "That boy's life played out in ways I never could have imagined, but it doesn't shake the foundation of my convictions. It demonstrates in a profound way that even our most solidly held truths are but ethereal and hopeful virtues to the less fortunate. That the integrity in our souls is terrifyingly similar to grains of sand in our hands. I knew Baxter Bishop. He was as innocent as it is possible for any of us to be, and he was placed on a path that wiser men would have failed with similar catastrophe. The man you scorn for whichever reasons you wish, walks a path shared by many and controlled by none." The old Russian wiped away a tear as he smiled at the rambunctious children outside. "It is our duty not to judge but to serve them. I do not cry because he is gone. I cry because I have lost a son, a son whose absence reminds me of something I am ashamed of having forgotten."

"Life is to be lived, not controlled;
and humanity is won by continuing
to play in face of certain defeat."
- Ralph Ellison -